THE *SECRET LIVES* OF *CHURCH LADIES*

DEESHA PHILYAW

THE *SECRET LIVES* OF *CHURCH LADIES*

WEST VIRGINIA UNIVERSITY PRESS
MORGANTOWN

First edition published 2020 by West Virginia University Press
Printed in the United States of America

ISBN
Paper 978-1-949199-73-4
Ebook 978-1-949199-74-1

Library of Congress Cataloging-in-Publication Data
Names: Philyaw, Deesha, author.
Title: The secret lives of church ladies / Deesha Philyaw.
Description: First edition. | Morgantown : West Virginia University Press, 2020.
Identifiers: LCCN 2020008805 | ISBN 9781949199734 (paperback) | ISBN 9781949199741 (ebook)
Classification: LCC PS3616.H479 A6 2020 | DDC 813/.6—dc23
LC record available at https://lccn.loc.gov/2020008805

Cover design by Stewart Williams.
Cover photo by Sewn Apart on Unsplash.
Book design by Than Saffel / WVU Press.

Stories in this collection appeared in slightly different form in the following publications:
"Eula," *Apogee Journal*, no. 9, Summer 2017; "Not Daniel," *Cheat River Review*, issue 10, Spring/Summer 2018; "Snowfall," *Baltimore Review*, Winter 2019; "How to Make Love to a Physicist," *Barrelhouse*, Special Issue: I've Got Love on My Mind: Black Women on Love, February 2020.

For Taylor and Peyton,
And for everyone trying to get free

Let it be known: I did not fall from grace.

I leapt

to freedom.

—Ansel Elkins,
"Autobiography of Eve"

CONTENTS

EULA

EULA BOOKS the suite in Clarksville, two towns over. I bring the food. This year it's sushi for me and cold cuts and potato salad for her. Nothing heavy. Just enough to sustain us. And I bring the champagne. This year, which like every year could be our last, I bring three bottles of André Spumante.

And I got us some noisemakers and year 2000 glasses to wear. The lenses are the two zeroes in the middle. For all we know, the Y2K bug will have us sitting in the dark one second after Dick Clark counts down in Times Square. But that's all right with me. Because that André sips just as well in the dark.

After we settle in, Eula digs into the potato salad and cold cuts. She's real particular about what she eats. About most things really. She likes things just so. She's a schoolteacher, like me, so we have to mind the details, though Eula minds them more closely than I do. But she can't tell I bought the potato salad from Publix, added some chopped boiled egg, mustard, pickle relish, and paprika, and put it in my red Tupperware bowl. She eats seconds, pats her belly, and tells me I outdid myself.

After we're finished eating and polishing off a bottle of the André, I start the shower. We like it boiling hot. The heat relaxes me, but I feel like it does something else for Eula. She stays in there long after I get out. Through the steamy shower door, I see her pink shower cap. Her head is bowed, and I wonder if she's asking God's forgiveness for stepping outside of His favor as she continues to wait on His provision.

—

By the time Eula and I turned thirty, ten years ago, we had been best friends for half our lives. We met in tenth grade, the only Black girls in our Honors English class. Eula had been new that year; her family moved down from North Carolina. She needed a friend, and I did too. We were daydreamers, planning our double Hawaiian wedding in the margins of our math notebooks. Our husbands would be railroad men like our fathers. We'd teach at the high school, join the Ladies Auxiliary at church, and be next-door neighbors. Our kids would play together.

But our thirtieth birthdays found us teaching at the high school and serving in the Ladies Auxiliary with no other parts of our daydreams realized. We celebrated Eula's birthday in her apartment, with too many wine coolers. She ended up in my lap, her skirt bunched up around her waist. I saw the white cotton panties between her thick brown thighs. She smelled like vanilla.

"Do you ever feel like you could just bust?" she asked me, her breath fruity and hot in my face.

I didn't answer, afraid that my honesty would send Eula running. But it didn't matter because she kept talking, begging me to touch her because no one had ever touched her down there. She had been a good girl, she told me. But I already knew that. As a teen, Eula hadn't sneaked behind her parents' backs as I had, curious, then disappointed, by what too-rough boys had to offer. And as a grown woman, she had not endured short-lived flings with men whose names weren't worth remembering, as I had. Eula had committed to praying and waiting for her Boaz, like Ruth in the Bible.

Eula is a true believer. She doesn't walk around with questions lingering in her throat like I do.

But that night, she slid my fingers inside those white cotton panties and forgot all about Boaz. We stayed up until we were slick with sweat. Later that morning, Eula tamped down regret with silence and coffee.

A month or so later, it was New Year's Eve, and Eula called to say that she'd booked a suite over in Clarksville. I brought white pizza and three bottles of Asti Spumante.

—

For Eula's birthday the next year, I planned a special dinner at my house for us. I went down to the fish market on Avery and got everything to make gumbo, her favorite dish. Eula liked my Grandma Pauline's gumbo, but without the okra, so that's how I made it. I cooked the night before Eula's birthday because Grandma always said the gumbo tasted better after it had a chance to sit in the Frigidaire for a day.

As I stirred the roux, which is my least favorite part of making gumbo because it requires patience, Eula called to ask if she could get a rain check on dinner. Reese, an attorney from our singles Bible study whom she'd been seeing for barely six months, wanted to take her out for her birthday. It was a surprise. Her words tumbled all over each other—*OhCarolettaIthinkhemightaskmetomarryhim*—and I just kept stirring that roux.

"You understand, right?" Eula had asked.

"Sure." I tried to think of something else to say that Eula would want to hear that wouldn't taste wounded and bitter in my mouth. But I couldn't come up with anything. It didn't matter anyway because Eula just prattled on, wondering how Reese could've managed to guess her ring size and what she would say to feign surprise when he popped the question.

In the end, both Eula and Reese got a surprise that night. Their romantic dinner at a rooftop restaurant (the original surprise) was interrupted by Reese's estranged wife.

Later, when Eula called to tell me what had happened, her fury just about leaped through the phone. I sat up in bed, listening, eating my second bowl of gumbo—with okra—another woman's husband snoring lightly beside me.

Over time, Eula had other Reeses, other almosts. But she would end up dismissing them as too old or too young. Too broke or too stupid. Or they would dismiss her once they realized they couldn't woo or pressure her into sleeping with them. Now'days, there are fewer and fewer Reeses, and they are less and less like Boaz with each passing year.

Sometimes I wonder if Eula finds fault with all these men because secretly she doesn't want any of them, and is just doing what's expected of her.

But these are the kinds of things Eula and I don't talk about.

—

After the shower, Eula puts on a white T-shirt and white cotton panties. She falls back on the king-size bed, floating on the crisp white sheets, plump pillows, and billowy comforter. Her hair is wrapped in a pink silk scarf. She takes a long drink, straight from the second bottle of André.

"Want some?" She holds the bottle out to me.

I crawl to her, from the foot of the bed. When I am next to her, she lifts the bottle to my mouth and then pours it down the front of my nightgown and giggles. "Let me get that," she says. She sets the bottle on the nightstand and pushes me back on the pillows. She straddles me, takes off my nightgown, and licks everywhere the champagne has touched.

—

About an hour later, I wake up, still drunk. Eula is up, drinking from the last bottle of André. She has muted the TV, but I can tell Dick Clark is introducing some little white girl with multicolored hair who had a hit early last year. Can't remember that child's name, and I guess it really doesn't matter. She can't dance to save her life and can't sing a lick.

"I have a New Year's resolution," Eula says, her eyes half-closed. "If I'm still alone come Valentine's Day, it will be the last one I spend without a man who belongs to me and me *only*."

"That's a pretty big resolution," I say, reaching

for the bottle. The sting of her saying she's alone doesn't roll off of me as quickly as it usually does. "What do you plan to do?"

"Like Pastor says: the Lord can't steer a parked car. I need to position myself to meet someone and prepare a place in my life for a husband."

"Meaning?"

"For starters, I been slacking off on going to Bible study. If I want a godly man, I need to be in the right places."

"You met Reese at Bible study . . ."

Eula rolls her eyes. "And I'm going to redecorate my house," she continues. "There's no room for a man, the way it is now. I want to make space for a husband."

"Sorta like feng shui."

"Feng what?"

"Never mind." I think about Eula being busy with all these man-finding activities while I do *what*? Entertain the occasional married boyfriend? Spend next New Year's Eve without her? I want a change too, but I have no plan.

"And I'm going to join the singles softball team at church," Eula says.

"You don't even like sports," I say, laughing.

"Laugh all you want." Eula adjusts the pillows behind her back. "But you need to get with the program too. Caroletta, don't you want someone to come home to? Someone to spend your life with? Don't you want to be happy?"

I look at Eula, her no-longer-fresh ringlets damp from the time spent between my legs. As I think about her question, something both cruel and pitiful churns inside me and threatens to spill out. Since when does she know or care anything about my happiness? Anything at all about it?

"I *am* happy," I say, coaxing my voice out to sound braver than I actually feel. "Right now. Right here. With you. And it doesn't have to be just this one night. We could—"

"Caroletta, I hope you haven't given up on finding you a husband. I'm on a mission, and you can be too." Eula sounds flat, like the world's most exhausted saleslady. She scoots away from me to the edge of the bed, looking at the TV.

"Eula, turn around and look at me. Please."

Eula shakes her head. To the TV, she says, "I don't want to die a virgin. Do you want to die a virgin?"

I guess I wait a beat too long to respond.

Eula whips around to face me. "You . . . *aren't*?"

I don't know what's funnier: that Eula thinks my forty-year-old ass hasn't had sex with a man in all these many years, or that she still considers us both virgins after all we've done together in those same years.

"Eula."

"You? With some dirty-ass man?" Eula clamps her hand over her mouth. In that moment, Sunday

School Teacher Eula snatches the reins from Biology Teacher Eula. "You aren't *clean*?"

"Eula!"

I expect her to grab her clothes and bolt. But she doesn't. She just sits on the bed, her body racked by sobs. "It wasn't supposed to be this way," she cries over and over again. I'm not even sure what *it* is. Me with men? Her with me? Life?

"Eula, what way was it supposed to be?"

She turns around and faces me. "I just want to be happy," she sobs. "And normal."

I want to close the gap between us, pull her to me and rock her until the tears stop, promise that everything will be okay, but I don't dare. I can't make everything okay, not the way she wants it.

"Normal according to who, Eula? Men who been dead for thousands of years? Who thought slavery was cool and treated women like property?"

"The Bible is the inerrant word of God," Eula whispers, as defiantly as a whisper can be.

"And you only believe that because of how another group of men interpret the first group of men. People say you're supposed to put your faith in God, not men. Do you think God wants you, or anybody, to go untouched for decades and decades? For their whole lives? Like Sister Stewart, Sister Wilson, Sister Hill, my mother after my father died—all those women at church who think they have to choose between pleasing

God and something so basic, so human as being held and known in the most intimate way. If God became human once—"

"If?" Eula says, spitting out the word.

"—then why would he make rules that force such a painful choice?"

"I don't question God."

"But maybe you should question the people who taught you this version of God. Because it's not doing you any favors."

Eula narrows her eyes at me. "You're not who I thought you were."

"You're not who you thought you were either."

—

On the TV, the Times Square crowd is going wild. It's almost time for the countdown. Eula and I are lying in the bed wearing only our year 2000 glasses. The noisemakers are still in the bag.

"I want to ring in the New Year in Times Square someday," Eula says, but her words are kind of mashed up because of the André.

"With me? Maybe we could go next year, instead of coming here."

Eula doesn't answer.

"Our friends down under in Sydney, Australia, were the first to ring in the New Year," Dick Clark says to a white woman in the crowd wearing a purple velvet Mad Hatter's hat. *"And other*

countries have celebrated as well without any loss of power or computer glitches. Do you think the Y2K bug was much ado about nothing?"

"I'm scared, Caroletta."

"I know."

Eula begins to whisper. I move closer to hear what she's saying and realize that she's praying.

When she says *amen*, I get up and walk to the foot of the bed and kneel down. Eula's toenails are painted the same pink as her scarf. I reach for her ankles and pull her toward me. She scoots on her butt until she's at the edge, her feet flat on the bed on either side of me. She spreads her knees apart. I push down gently on the inside of her thighs, until she is open, like an altar.

10-9-8 . . .

I am speaking in tongues.

4-3-2 . . .

Eula has her prayers and I have mine.

NOT-DANIEL

I PARKED in the shadows behind the hospice center, and waited. I held a box of condoms on my lap, Magnum XLs. It was like being sixteen again, except this time I bought the condoms instead of relying on the boy. This time the boy was a man I had mistaken for someone I'd gone to junior high with when our paths first crossed two weeks before at the main entrance of the hospice center. I was coming, he was going. I thought he was Daniel McMurray so I stared longer than I should have, and he stared back. Later that evening, I'd run into him again coming out of the room across from my mother's. His mother had breast cancer, mine ovarian.

I checked my phone. *10:27.* I'd timed the Walmart run for the condoms pretty well. Not-Daniel would be down in three minutes. To throw Nurse Irie, the night nurse, off the trail, we never left or returned to the floor at the same time. Her name wasn't really Irie, but I called her that behind her back because she was Jamaican. She was also mean as a snake. I had complained to the head of the center about her, suggesting that her brusque manner was better suited for the morgue. But Nurse Irie liked Not-Daniel. She didn't cop an attitude when he asked questions about his mother's care. He told me she even joked with him late one night as he walked around the floor in his skimpy running shorts: "Boi, you keep walking around here in those itty bitty tings, someone might mess around and give you a sponge bath."

Nurse Irie was not a stupid woman. Perhaps she would put two and two together and figure out that Not-Daniel and I were . . . what were we? What do you call it when your mothers are hospice neighbors and the nights are endless and sleepless and here's someone else who spent the day talking to insurance companies and creditors and banks and pastors and relatives and friends, some more well-intentioned than others? Someone else who is the dutiful son to your dutiful daughter, another family's chief shit handler, bail bondsman, maid, chauffeur, therapist, career advisor, ATM. Here's someone else who both welcomes and dreads death as it loiters in the wings, an unpredictable actor.

What do you call it when that someone else wears a wedding band but never mentions his wife by name? A wife and two kids back home in the next state over. Don't ask, don't tell.

At exactly ten thirty, Not-Daniel tapped the passenger-side window. For a few moments, we sat in silence the way we always did at first. Sometimes I would cry, sometimes he would too, because we could out here, beyond the reach of our mothers' Jesus, nurses on autopilot, empty platitudes, and garbage theology about God's will disguised as comfort. And then eventually, one of us would speak.

But this night . . . how to begin? Pick up where we'd left off the night before? When yet another rambling conversation about funerals and selfish siblings suddenly became kissing, became my T-shirt off, became my nipples in Not-Daniel's mouth.

This is how we began: Not-Daniel took the box of condoms from me, removed one, and then set the box on the dashboard next to my phone. Then he set his phone on the dashboard. I knew his ringer volume, like mine, was on the highest setting, because the call, that call, could come at any moment. Then he took my face in his hands and looked at me. I dropped my eyes.

"No," he said. "I need you to be . . . here. All of you. Here."

Lifting my eyes to meet his, I felt like Sisyphus

pushing that rock. In his eyes, I saw *wifekidsdyingmother*. I blinked, and blinked again, until my vision cleared.

In the back seat, Not-Daniel undressed me, undressed himself, and then buried his face between my legs. I reached over my head, clutched the door behind me, and cried as I came over and over again.

By the time Not-Daniel put on the condom and pulled me to my knees, my legs were limp and useless. He turned me away from him, pressed his palm against the center of my back and pushed me forward. He draped his body over mine and entered me. He was rough, but not unkind.

I wondered whether he was thinking what I was thinking: what if one of our mothers dies while we're down here rutting around, as my grandmother would say?

But in the cramped space of the back seat and of our grief and our need, there was no room for guilt or fear. Only relief.

And that's what I told Not-Daniel when we were both spent, our damp backs sticking to the leather seat.

"*Relieved*?" He frowned and then smiled. "Relieved? Then I failed to deliver the goods."

"No, no," I said. "You . . . delivered the goods. The goods were delivered. And received. But I do have a question . . ."

"Shoot."

"Were you worried that one of them would die while we were down here?"

"Thought never crossed my mind."

"Really?"

"Really. Listen, I can either deliver the goods, or I can think about my mama, dying or not. I can't do both."

And then I laughed, even though I felt like I shouldn't have. Even though nothing was as it should be.

DEAR SISTER

—

DEAR JACKIE:

I've started this letter about five different times in five different ways. Finally I just told myself you're either going to read it or you're not, and it's not going to come down to how I write it. It's all about who you are and what you've been through and what, if anything, it means to you to share a father with my sisters Renee, Kimba, Tasheta, and me. Maybe it means nothing. Maybe your life has been just fine without our father in it, which I hope is the case. Maybe it means everything, and you have longed to know him and struggled because you didn't. Either way, you have a right to know that our father Wallace "Stet" Brown died last week of a massive stroke.

As far as we know, you never met our father. The last time he saw you, you were an infant. If that's the case, and if it's any consolation: you didn't miss much. (Tasheta, our baby sister, asked me to tell you that. We're all sitting around at Grandma's house, and everyone is talking at once, telling me what I should write to you. I'm mostly ignoring them. They picked me to write this because I shoot straight and don't mince words. But I also have tact, unlike Tasheta.)

Oh! In case you're wondering, we always just called it "Grandma's house," even though Granddaddy lived here too, when he was alive. He died of a heart attack in 2002, God rest his soul. You would have loved him. Everybody did. Always had a joke or funny story to tell. He was good people, just like Grandma. They lost their kids to the street or hard living, one way or another, even though they tried their best to raise them right. But some people just go their own way, you know?

Anyway, back to Stet. Tasheta is right. You didn't miss much. Stet—everybody but Grandma called him "Stet" because back in high school, he wore a Stetson—Stet wasn't much of a daddy. Each of us girls had a different kind of relationship with him, none of them healthy and none of them what we needed it to be.

Kimba is the oldest, and she's the peacekeeper. She called our father "Wallace," but she mostly pretended he didn't exist. Over the years, she's kept Tasheta and Renee from strangling each other. She went to Harvard. Her mother (Jan) and my mother had been friends . . . before

Stet. But by the time Kimba and I were in elementary school, they had put their differences aside and raised us together like sisters. My mama said, "Y'all gon' need each other one day. Me and Jan aren't always going to be here. And you sure as hell can't count on your daddy."

Anyway . . . Kimba lives in Philadelphia now, with her husband and two kids. Your niece and nephew. She's the only one of us with kids, and she's the quietest one. Like I said, the peacekeeper. She flew down as soon as Renee called her with the news, and she's helping out with Grandma. But I can tell she really wants to get the hell out of town and back to her life.

Speaking of Grandma . . . I don't think Alzheimer's has fully set in yet, but she's on her way. She can't always remember our names, but she knows that her baby boy died. And she's sad about it. She's been crying off and on. At seventy-five, she's outlived her husband and all but one of her children, our Uncle Bird who moved in to take care of her when Granddaddy died.

Last week, after Kimba arrived, we met up for dinner at Grandma's. Her neighbors and the people from her church had dropped off food. We had food for days: fried chicken, baked chicken, macaroni and cheese, greens, deviled eggs, potato salad, black-eyed peas and rice, pound cake.

So we were sitting there eating and whatnot, and Grandma says, "Which one-a y'all pregnant?"

She waved a chicken leg around like a pointer. "I dreamed about fish near 'bout every night this week."

We been hearing about Grandma's fishy dreams all our lives. With seven children, nineteen grandchildren (including you), eight great-grands, and three great-great-grands, Grandma has dreamed about fish a lot.

"Somebody 'round here pregnant," she muttered.

Renee, Kimba, and I just looked at each other and shook our heads. "It's not us, Grandma," Renee said. (Tasheta hadn't gotten here yet; she's always late.)

Anyway . . . Grandma and her fishy dreams announced the existence of every one of her children, grandchildren, great-grandchildren, and great-great-grandchildren. ("Except for Khalil," she always reminded us. "You know Derrick never brang that girl around until that baby was two weeks old. And you know she had the nerve to get an attitude because I told her she shouldn't have that baby out so soon with no shoes on his feet, no hat, nothing. I don't care if it was June." June 1986, but Grandma still talks about that girl and that baby like it was yesterday. Khalil is nineteen and is a daddy his own self now!)

If Grandma dreams about fish, there is a baby baking inside someone in her life. Everybody talks about how she's only been wrong once, and they chalk it up to the fact that she was in the hospital at the time from complications related to her diabetes and was probably just having wild dreams because she was sick. But Jackie, I'm going to tell you a secret that only our sisters know: I knew that wasn't true. I felt more guilty about ruining Grandma's track record in the eyes of the family than I did about the abortion in the eyes of God. Fifteen years later, and Grandma still complaining about how "the sugar is even worser than them doctors realize. Messing around with folks' dreams . . ." But I don't have the heart to tell her what I did.

But this time, it's really not me who's pregnant. I know for a fact that it ain't me, because I ain't been with nobody in almost a year. Because men are tiring, and I don't have the energy. Are you married? Do you have kids?

Anyway . . . Maybe it's one of our cousins, or second cousins? Or Tasheta. But she gets those Depo shots . . .

I know who ain't pregnant for sure: our middle sister, Renee. Because she is probably still a virgin. Renee is definitely the most delusional one of us when it comes to Stet. She is my full blood sister. (I don't like to think about it, but I guess my mama felt like being the same fool twice where Stet was concerned.) Renee and me don't have much else in common. Like the situation with Stet. When we were in grade school, she was always telling people that Stet and Mama were married, that he took us on Bahamas cruises every year, and that Stet bought her a Barbie Dreamhouse for Christmas. Every year it was some big gift. Meanwhile Stet went on Bahamas cruises every year all right—with his girlfriends. And he never once bought us gifts. All we could count on him for was broken promises, late child support (if there was any at all), and summers at Grandma's house. Those summers were the only good thing I can say about him, and really they weren't about him because he'd be in the streets the whole time we were there.

But none of that fazed Renee. She bought that man a card and a gift every birthday, every Father's Day, every Christmas. Like he was Father of the Year or something. Mama would ask me if I wanted to get him something too. No, ma'am. That's just what I told her. *No, ma'am.*

So Tasheta and me, we fell in line somewhere in the space between Kimba and Renee. Like a daughter purgatory where you don't expect him to get you anything for your birthday or Christmas, ever, but it still hurts like hell every time he doesn't.

One time, one Father's Day, Renee and I were at church with Grandma. Renee was ten, I was thirteen. Stet had promised Grandma that he would come to church. He was always promising Grandma he would come to church. Renee and I sat on either side of Grandma in the second pew or the right side of the sanctuary, where Grandma always sat. Renee just kept turning around and turning around, looking at the door at the back of the church. I know she was thinking Stet was going to walk in any minute. She was holding a gift, a pack of socks she'd gotten for him and wrapped herself in Christmas paper. Pastor got to the end of the sermon, and Renee just kept turning around, turning around. Grandma patted her knee and hugged her close. But she kept looking back.

Then the pastor did the altar call, inviting anyone who wanted to ask Jesus into their heart to come forward. And then he asked all the fathers to come forward to commit or recommit their lives to their children. Renee watched all those men come forward and kneel at the altar and promise to be good fathers to their children. Then she looked back one last time, and the tears started.

On the way out the church, she threw the socks in the garbage can. If I could've taken that pain away from her that day, I would have. But I couldn't. All I could say to her is what I'd heard our mama say about Stet, "He doesn't deserve us." I knew it was true—he didn't deserve us. But I don't think Renee ever believed that. I don't think she's ever learned what she deserves, what she's worth.

—

So I had to take a little break from writing you. Fixed me another plate. Thinking about that Father's Day at church years ago made me wonder what Father's Days were like for you, and all the other days as well. Is it better to have the one big hurt of your father not being around and not all those little hurts that come when he disappoints you? Or is it better to have a piece of a father, hurts and all?

Well, it's not like any of us got to choose in the beginning. But we do get to decide how much space to give him now.

I really hope that this letter doesn't make things harder for you. It wasn't our idea to reach out at first. Growing up we'd heard things here and there, that there was another sister, but we didn't pay it no never mind. But while we were sitting here a few days ago, Grandma's neighbor Miss Margaret stopped by with a sweet potato pie.

She said, "Didn't y'all have another sister . . . the fat one?"

We had no idea what she was talking about.

"She was over here visiting a few years back. Was married to some man from up North."

"Oh, that was me, Miss Margaret," Kimba said. "My husband is from Philadelphia. And I was pregnant the last time I was here."

"No, you were just fat. I remember when you were pregnant."

I swear, old people stay saying slick shit because they know we can't shake them. Kimba just looked at me like, "Is this bitch for real?"

And Miss Margaret kept talking. "And there was another one of y'all . . . another girl Stet had."

"We never met her," Renee said, a little too quickly.

"Well, she has a right to know," Miss Margaret said. She turned to Grandma. "Don't you think she has a right to know, Mae?"

Grandma looked up from her piece of pie. "Who?"

Miss Margaret shook her head. "Never mind."

Then Tasheta came in, loud and on the phone, as usual. "Girl!" she was saying to someone, "Tell him you not a mind reader. He better speak up if he wants to be down. Closed mouths don't get head!" And then she cracked up at her own wordplay. "I'm serious . . . Look. You know how they say, 'No child left behind'? I say, 'No nigga left undrained.' "

"Tasheta!" Renee jumped up from the table. "That's disgusting. Show some respect."

Tasheta held her open palm inches away from Renee's face. Dismissed. She still wore hospital scrubs, and she'd pulled her microbraids up into a bun.

Miss Margaret turned up her nose. "Lord

Jesus, let me get up out of here. Mae, I will talk to you later. Take care."

Tasheta ended her call and kissed Grandma on the cheek. "Hey, Grandma."

"Lord knows where that mouth has been," Miss Margaret mumbled on her way out the door.

"Thank you for stopping by, Miss Margaret," Kimba said following her out onto the front porch. "And for the pie. We'll see you at the service on Saturday."

That scene pretty much tells you everything you need to know about Tasheta. Well, that and the fact that she and one of her married boyfriends just celebrated their fifth anniversary.

Kimba asked Tasheta, "Do you ever remember Wallace talking about another daughter of his?"

Renee huffed. "Come on, Grandma. I'm going to run you a bath. It's getting late."

Tasheta thought about Kimba's question between bites of macaroni and cheese that she was eating straight from the baking dish. "Nah," she said. "Doesn't ring a bell."

"Miss Margaret thinks we should get in touch with her. But we don't know anything about her."

"Did you ask Uncle Bird?"

Tasheta is wild, but she's also smart. Her mom used to be a stripper, but she made sure Tasheta stayed in her books and went to college like the rest of us. She's a nurse, Kimba's a professor, Renee's a kindergarten teacher, and I'm a program director at a social services nonprofit. What do you do?

So . . . I volunteered to go talk to Uncle Bird (real name: Bert) who was back in the bedroom he used to share with Stet when they were boys. Uncle Bird's eyes were red from crying. Stet's passing really shook him up. That was his big brother and best friend.

Uncle Bird couldn't recall your name, and he could only remember your mama's first name. But he said he remembered your mom coming by Grandma's house a few times, and he saw you once when you were a baby.

"Your daddy was something else," Uncle Bird said. He was stretched out on his old twin bed. I sat on Stet's. "Nothing got past him. You know back in the day, I used to do my dirt. And he'd call me on it. We were sitting around drankin' with some fellas one time. I had just gotten back from Miami, handling some business, but I wasn't saying what that business was. Stet pointed at me from across the table and said, 'Only a coupla of things a nigga is driving to Miami for . . . to buy some dope, see some kids, or make some more kids.' "

Uncle Bird laughed. "And I said, 'Nigga, I *know* you not talking about somebody having a bunch of kids. You the only motherfucker I know describe his kids like a Spades hand.' " Uncle Bird mimicked my father's slow drawl: " 'Uhhh . . . I got five and a possible.' "

We both laughed. And then Uncle Bert was crying again. Grief is like that. He hadn't just lost Stet. He'd also lost his four other siblings, all too soon. To drugs, violence, or both. We barely got to know our aunts and uncles.

When I got back to the dining room, Tasheta was pouring tequila shots for herself and Kimba. She went and got another glass and poured me one too.

You probably won't be surprised to know that Renee didn't want us to find you. (And that she turned her nose up at the tequila.) She said you'd probably come sniffing around thinking Stet left some money. I reminded her that Stet didn't have a pot to piss in or a window to throw it out of when he died. Don't mind her. I told you, she's delusional. After all these years, she's still the doting daughter. She used to go over there and grocery shop and cook for him every week. She spent Friday nights over there watching TV like an old person. She was the one who found him dead on the bathroom floor. I asked her once if she was dating. She said she believes in courting, not dating, and that someday, the man God chose for her would find her. I wondered how he was supposed to find her since she didn't go anywhere but to work and Stet's house. Did she think the cable guy or Stet's building super could be the man God chose?

While we were sitting there sipping, Tasheta's phone rang. Kimba glanced down and read the name on the caller ID: " 'Rectal Rooter'? Tasheta, what in the world?"

Tasheta snatched up the phone. "Mind your business!" She went into the living room and proceeded to have another loud conversation.

Renee looked like she was going to pass out. Kimba and I just took another shot.

When Tasheta came back to the dining room, Renee was still pissy. "Tasheta, even if you don't have any self-respect, you should at least respect the sanctity of other people's marriages." Tasheta took another shot. "I respect their marriages," she said, slapping her glass down on the table. "Until they don't want me to."

Kimba giggled, and I lost it. We all busted out laughing—except for Renee, of course.

"You two condone her behavior?" Renee asked.

Kimba, loosened up by the tequila, said, "It's not for me to condone or not condone. Tash is a grown-ass woman."

"Don't even bother, Kimba," Tasheta said. "When you're not here, I just ignore Miss Holier-Than-Thou."

"Back to the subject at hand . . ." Renee said. "It's for the best that Uncle Bert couldn't remember that other girl's name. Everything happens for a reason."

"Jesus Christ, I swear your native tongue is 'Cliché.' "

"Don't you—"

"—take the Lord's name in vain, blah, blah, blah. Do you realize you cling to an imaginary white daddy because your flesh-and-blood daddy wasn't shit? Well, guess what. Your imaginary white daddy ain't shit either. If he was, he would've given you a real daddy that was worth a damn."

Renee took a deep breath and turned her back to Tasheta and addressed the rest of us. "As I was saying: it's for the best. She isn't really one of us anyway."

"One of us?" Tasheta laughed. "And who are we exactly? Except a bunch of women fathered by the same old deadbeat nigga with a thing for barely legal girls. She most definitely is *one of us*."

"I *mean*"—Renee whipped around again to face Tasheta—"she didn't know our father like we did. And even though you did not respect him in life, at least show some respect for the dead."

Tasheta began to speak, but Kimba cut her off. "To your corners, ladies. You are working my last good nerve." She rubbed her temples.

Tasheta giggled. "Girl, that's just the tequila."

Renee said, "Scripture says, 'Honor thy father and thy mother—' "

"*Honor thy father*?" Tasheta yelled. "When did that motherfucker ever honor you? Or me? Or Kimba? Or Nichelle? Or anybody but his own trifling self? I ain't honoring shit."

"Blasphemer!" Renee screamed and covered her ears.

Tasheta laughed. "Are you fucking kidding me right now?"

"Both of you!" Kimba hissed. "Keep it down. Grandma and Uncle Bird are resting."

Renee lowered her voice. "I know one thing. You better not make a scene at the funeral."

Tasheta tilted her head to the side. "Or what?"

(You might be interested to know that Tasheta is the only one of us who knows how to fight. Kimba will debate you until you cry uncle. Renee will pray for you. And I'm just gonna talk a lot of shit from a distance.)

"Or . . . or I will have you escorted from the church."

"Yeah, okay. Good luck with that."

"I'm serious, Tasheta. Funerals are to honor the dead and comfort the living. If you can't respect that, you need to stay away."

"Listen, I know you think you're in charge and you were his favorite and all of that. You can have that. But you don't run me. You. Don't. Run. Shit. Here." Tasheta punctuated each word of her last sentence with a clap.

"Can we call a truce?" Kimba asked.

"No!" Tasheta and Renee said.

"Renee," I said. "Stop carrying on like we're some kind of great dynasty and Stet was some kind of patriarch. And if you're going to quote Scripture, quote the whole thing. 'Honor your father and mother—which is the first commandment with a promise—so that it may go well with you and that you may enjoy long life on the earth.' Girl, I get it. You are trying to get that crown in heaven. And you wanted desperately for that man to love you back. And maybe he did. But respect the fact that the rest of us didn't want what you wanted and didn't get whatever it is you think you got from him."

Renee folded her arms and began to cry. She looked so much like her ten-year-old self that Father's Day in church, I almost backed down. Almost.

"And," I said, "if we're going to keep it really real, the next verse says, 'Fathers, don't exasperate your children; instead, bring them up in the training and instruction of the Lord.' "

"In other words," Tasheta said, "if you weren't beating him over the head with Scripture, leave me the fuck alone about it."

"And you . . ." I turned to Tasheta. "We are more than just some deadbeat's kids. We're sisters. We don't always get along, but we've always had each other's backs. I'm not going to wear black and sit up in that church because he was some great father. We all know he wasn't. I'm going because I love Grandma and Uncle Bird and Renee and Kimba and your messy ass. Stet was our connection, but it's not like we haven't spent our whole lives together, 99 percent of the time without him. We spent whole summers in this house, playing all day in that tiny-ass front yard because Grandma wouldn't let us out the gate. Remember?"

Kimba and Tasheta nodded and started cracking up. Even Renee cracked a smile.

Kimba said, "Remember that time we came in from playing, and Uncle Bird said, 'Gotdamn, y'all smell like a pack of billy goats!' "

"And Grandma hit him in the back with the rolled up newspaper for cussing in her house?" Renee said, rolling her eyes in Tasheta's direction.

We laughed some more, then we sat there, quiet for the first time in forever, remembering. There had been good times and close times. Those summers at Grandma's. Spending the night at each other's houses during the school year. Swapping clothes. Trips to Disney World. Worrying over boys. Complaining about our mothers. Doing each other's hair. Proms. Graduations. Kimba's wedding.

And Stet had had nothing to do with any of that. Because he was a man who took without giving, he left us nothing to grieve.

Tasheta broke the silence. She stood up and made herself a plate to go. "I got work in the morning. I'm out," she said. She grabbed her keys and purse, and hugged everyone goodbye except Renee.

At this point, you may be thinking that this situation is a hot mess, and there's no way in the world you want to have anything to do with us. But I promise you: we are the best sisters you could ask for. Let me tell you what happened next.

The next time we were all together was for the limo ride to the funeral. Renee put all of us sisters in one limo, and Grandma, Uncle Bird, and Kimba's husband and kids in the other.

Renee and Tasheta were still in the midst of a cold war, but at least it was cold. Tasheta showed up at Grandma's house the morning of the funeral in a backless black dress and clear heels, but agreed to wear a blazer Renee pulled out of the trunk of her car.

The funeral was . . . a funeral. Renee, Grandma, and Uncle Bird cried. Kimba's kids were restless; her mom tried to keep them occupied with snacks. My mother sat in the last pew; I didn't see her, but that's where she told me she would be. A bunch of Stet's friends who knew nothing about him as a father stood up and talked about what a great friend he was. The choir sang two songs. The pastor spoke of my grandparents' faithfulness as a covering on the lives of their children and their children's children, which I suppose was the most he could say. And then he did the thing pastors always do at the funeral of someone who hadn't darkened the church's door in a few decades: reminded mourners of their own mortality and where they are likely to spend eternity if they don't get right with Jesus.

Jesus and I got right at an altar call years ago, so I basically zoned out at that point. Stet and I had also made our peace a long time ago too. I stopped expecting him to be a father, and he stopped expecting me to be Renee. When the usher came to lead us out of the sanctuary when the service was over, I was beyond ready to go.

At the graveside, we sisters gathered round Grandma and Uncle Bird as the casket was lowered into the ground. After everyone dispersed to head back to the church for the repast, I stood next to the grave, alone. I wasn't ready to be with people just yet.

But of course, Black people can never just leave you alone. A light-skinned man with jowls and graying hair walked over and stood next to me. "I'm so sorry for your loss," he said.

"Thank you."

"I was your daddy's friend. Chauncey?" Chauncey waited for some sign of recognition on my face. When there was none, he just kept talking, wagging his finger at me.

"You know, your daddy always talked about

you. Bragged about you. Always getting straight As in school. Going off to college and whatnot. Yale!"

"That's . . . not me. That's my sister, Kimba. And she went to Harvard."

"Oh, well, you know, alla y'all made him proud . . . Yessir, mmmh mmmh *mmmh*! Stet got some really beautiful daughters." Chauncey rubbed my shoulder, and I shuddered at his touch. I'm sure he felt it, but he kept on rubbing. My skin went clammy beneath the fabric of my suit jacket.

"Real beautiful girls," he said.

It took a few seconds for Chauncey's words to register as a compliment. Then it took a few seconds more for this to register as a highly inappropriate compliment, given the circumstances and the way his hand lingered on me.

"So whatchu doin' later on?" he asked.

I pulled away. I squinted. This couldn't be happening. "You've got five seconds to get the fuck away from me," I said, "before I start screaming for my uncle to come over here and stomp a mudhole in you. Five . . ."

Chauncey backed away.

In the limo, I was quiet. I figured everyone would just think the weight of the day was on me. But not Tasheta. I told you that girl is smart.

"NiNi, what's the matter?"

I swallowed hard and told them what had happened.

"Oh, hell, no," Renee said. "That motherfucker . . ." We all stared at her.

At the repast, I sat with Grandma, Uncle Bird, Kimba and her crew, and my mother. Ladies from the church brought us heaping plates of food and cups of fruit punch.

At the next table, I saw Tasheta sitting across from Chauncey, smiling and nodding. From what I could make out, he was once again talking about Stet's beautiful daughters. Renee joined them and set a plate of food and a cup of punch in front of Chauncey. He kept on talking, and Renee and Tasheta kept on smiling and nodding.

And then Chauncey took a long drink of his fruit punch.

And screamed.

He clawed at his throat. He broke into a sweat, and his eyes filled with tears. Some of the ladies from the church rushed over to help. Renee and Tasheta floated over to our table with their plates, sat down, and kept eating.

"What happened to Chauncey?" Uncle Bird asked.

"Maybe he put a little too much hot sauce on his chicken. Or something," Renee said. "Grandma, can I get you anything?"

"Oh, no, baby," Grandma said. "I'm good. Just need to find out who in here pregnant. I keep having them fish dreams . . ."

It was a long day.

And this was a long letter. But we didn't just want you to know that Stet died. We also wanted you to know *us*. Even Renee. She'll come around. When Uncle Bird finally remembered your mother's last name, she pouted a little, but she's just as curious about you as the rest of us are.

And Kimba says that if you're ever in Philadelphia, let her know. All of our addresses and phone numbers are below.

And Uncle Bird said to tell you that he's got room in his heart for one more niece.

And I've got room in mine for one more sister.

Finally, Tasheta wants to know if you prefer brown or white liquor.

Your sister,
Nichelle

P.S. Grandma wants to know if you're pregnant.

PEACH COBBLER

MY MOTHER'S peach cobbler was so good, it made God himself cheat on his wife. When I was five, I hovered around my mother in the kitchen, watching, close enough to have memorized all the ingredients and steps by the time I was six. But not too close to make her yell at me for being in the way. And not close enough to see the exact measurements she used. She never wrote the recipe down. Without having to be told, I learned not to ask questions about that cobbler, or about God. I learned not to say anything at all about him hunching over our kitchen table every Monday eating plate after plate of peach cobbler, and then disappearing into the bedroom I shared with my mother.

I became a silent student of my mother and her cobbler-making ways. Even when I was older and no longer believed that God and Reverend Troy Neely were one and the same, I still longed to perfect the sweetness and textures of my mother's cobbler. My mother, who fed me TV dinners, baked a peach cobbler with fresh peaches every Monday, her day off from the diner where she waited tables. She always said Sunday was her Saturday and Monday was her Sunday. What I knew was that none of her days were for me.

And for many of those Mondays off and on during my childhood, God (to my child's mind) would stop by and eat an entire 8 x 8 pan of cobbler. My mother never ate any of the cobbler herself; she said she didn't like peaches. She would shoo me out of the kitchen before God could offer me any, but I doubted he would have offered even if I'd sat right down next to him. God was an old fat man, like a Black Santa, and I imagined my mother's peach cobbler contributing to his girth.

Some Mondays, God would arrive after dinner and leave as I lay curled up on the couch watching *Little House on the Prairie* in the living room. Other times my mother and God would already be in the bedroom when I got home from school. I could hear moaning and pounding, like a board hitting a wall, as soon as I entered the house. I would shut the front door quietly behind me and tiptoe down the hall to listen outside the bedroom door. "Oh, God! Oh, God! Oh, God!" my mother would cry. I could hear God too, his voice low and growly, saying, "Yes, yes, yes!"

Even before he started coming by on Mondays, I had suspected that Pastor Neely, the pastor of Hope in Christ Baptist Church, was God. He was big, black, and powerful, as I imagined God to be. My very first Easter speech, memorized in kindergarten during Sunday School, was "Jesus is the Son of God," but I didn't find it odd that Black God could have a blue-eyed, blond son. Pastor Neely was dark, his wife was pale, and their son, Trevor, who was around my age, had gray eyes and wasn't too much darker than the Jesus whose picture hung all over church. Plus, midway through every Sunday service, Pastor Neely, his wife, and Trevor stood in the front of the sanctuary and collected a love offering from the congregation as the choir sang "I Love You (Lord Today)." So it was easy for me to deduce that Pastor Neely was the "Lord." My mother's cries of passion through our bedroom door confirmed it.

I enjoyed the theater of Pastor Neely's Sunday sermons. From the pulpit, he thundered and roared at the congregation about God's wrath and judgment. And when he intoned about God's goodness and mercy, he wrapped his arms around himself and rocked. Then he stepped down from the pulpit and prowled the aisles of the sanctuary, energized and excited to tell us what he called the Good News. For a big man, he moved with surprising ease and grace. By the time he got to the altar call, most of the women and some of the men would be up on their feet, swaying and crying out. But not my mother. She stayed seated, her face unreadable as usual.

Pastor and First Lady Neely were the opposite of Jack Sprat and his wife. He, thick and corpulent. She, gangly and gaunt, like a child's stick figure drawing. During the love offering, she stood as straight and stiff as an arrow. Her straight brown hair hung past her shoulders, and I thought she was a white woman until years later, when I saw her up close for the first time, at her front door.

Like many of the church ladies, First Lady Neely wore a wide-brimmed hat, but hers hung low and almost obscured her eyes. But I could see enough of her to know that she did not have big, begging eyes like my mother; she was not beautiful like my mother. She did not have my mother's round breasts and full hips, the kind that excited strange men on the street. Men my mother called "dirty motherfuckers" when they said nasty things to her as we walked past. First Lady Neely probably never walked anywhere. I saw her stepping out of a pink Cadillac in the church parking lot one day. I heard one of the church ladies standing nearby say she had earned that car selling Mary Kay.

Pastor Neely always drove a luxury car, a new one each year, gifts from the congregation. He parked it in our backyard, which was adjacent to the woods. Our house sat alone at the dead end of a gravel road. The nearest neighbor was a half a mile away, near my bus stop.

One day, in second grade, I ran that whole half mile home, excited to share some good news with my mother. I burst into the house, threw my backpack on the couch, and ran straight into the kitchen, breathless.

Pastor Neely sat at the table, hunched over. It was a Monday. He looked up from his plate of cobbler and said hello in that fake, forced way that drags out the *o*—the way people say it when they don't enjoy talking to children. I said hello back, and he went right back to his cobbler. He ate surprisingly small spoonfuls, slowly. His full lips, slightly parted and glistening, made me think of the kissing I saw on TV and the movies. The spoon practically disappeared in his bear paw of a hand. His fingers resembled the thick sausages my mother made for breakfast sometimes on Sunday morning.

My mother leaned against the counter near the back door with her arms folded, watching Pastor Neely eat. She looked pleased—not particularly happy, but pleased. And yet she watched him so intently she also appeared ready to rush and block the door if he tried to leave.

"Mama!" I said, still gasping to catch my breath. "Guess what!"

"What?" She never took her eyes off the pastor.

"Latasha Wilson invited me to her birthday slumber party. Can I go?" The talk at school was Latasha Wilson lived in a two-story house and had a pink canopy Barbie bed. Her hair was always neatly pressed and pulled into a high ponytail of shiny, spiraling curls. Her father worked at a bank. The birthday party invitation, which I'd shoved down inside the front of my shirt, smelled like bubble gum. Latasha smelled like bubble gum. I bet her house smelled like bubble gum too. I couldn't wait to find out.

"No," my mother said.

I bit down on the "why not" that almost slipped out of my mouth. My mother's eyes were still on Pastor Neely. His eyes were still on the cobbler. My eyes filled with tears.

"Go on and change out of your school clothes," my mother said.

Tears spilled down my cheeks as I backed out of the kitchen. At first I stood in the hallway out of sight instead of going to the bedroom to change. Normally I did what my mother told me to do. But at that moment, I was too crushed.

I peeked around the corner. My mother had sat down at the table, across from Pastor Neely. She couldn't see me peeking, but Pastor Neely suddenly looked up from the cobbler, right at me! I quickly moved out of sight, bracing myself. But instead of ratting me out, Pastor Neely asked my mother a question: "Why won't you let the girl go to the party?"

I peeked around the corner again.

My mother sighed. "Because I like to keep to myself and she needs to learn to keep to herself too. It's better that way. You go accepting invitations, then people expect an invitation in return. Then you got people coming in your house, looking at what you have and what you don't have. And the next thing you know, your business is all over town." My mother ran her fingertips along the edge of the table and smiled to herself. "And I'm sure you can understand not wanting to have your business all over town."

Pastor Neely didn't say anything. He just took another bite of cobbler and shook his head.

"And besides . . ." my mother said, "I'm trying to raise her to be satisfied with what she has. I know that lil girl Latasha's mama and her daddy. Went to school with them. They've always been flashy, like to show off. He used to drive her around in his daddy's Lincoln until his daddy bought him a Mustang. At sixteen years old. They got money and all that come with it. So you know Latasha don't want for nothing and that birthday party is going to be over the top."

"I don't know these people," Pastor Neely said, "but if the Lord has blessed them, and they want to celebrate their child's birthday and invite your child to share in it, I don't see the problem." It was strange hearing Pastor Neely talk about the Lord outside of his pulpit. Instead of that scary, booming voice, he sounded like a regular person. A regular person who might convince my mother to let me go to Latasha Wilson's birthday party. I crossed my fingers on both hands.

My mother sat up straighter in her chair. When she spoke, it was slowly, as if she were trying to choose her words carefully. "They can raise their child however they see fit. But I'm not going to raise mine to go through life expecting it to be sweet, when for her, it ain't going to be. The sooner she learns to accept what is and what ain't, the better. She get a taste of that sweetness, she's going to want it so bad, she'll grow up and settle for crumbs of it."

Pastor Neely glanced at me again, shook his head, and ate the last bite of cobbler.

I ducked back out of sight and uncrossed my fingers. My eyes filled with tears again. Without looking, I knew my mother would whisk away the empty cobbler pan, the pastor's plate, and the spoon. I knew she would dunk them in the soapy dishwater in the sink, like she always did, so that I couldn't even sneak a taste of the remnants later.

"You got the best cobbler in the world right here," I heard Pastor Neely say, Latasha Wilson's birthday party invitation apparently forgotten.

He said this all the time. And because I believed he was a kind of Black Santa, I imagined him preaching at church on Sunday, traveling the whole world Tuesday through Saturday to try other mothers' peach cobblers, but always coming back to my mother's on Monday.

I went and changed out of my school clothes, then sat on the couch, unsure of what to do with this new feeling toward my mother: anger.

I heard them go into our bedroom and shut the door. I got up to put a TV dinner in the oven. Sometimes my mother remembered to put one in, sometimes she didn't. The fried chicken, mashed potatoes, corn, and warm brownie was my favorite. I always ate the brownie first, while it was still gooey in the middle.

Sometimes Pastor Neely and my mother would be in the bedroom for minutes, sometimes an hour. Always there was laughter when they came out. My mother would be laughing at some joke I hadn't heard, and she would wish Pastor Neely a good night. And he would laugh and thank her again for the peach cobbler.

I remember the laughter because the silence in our house between visits from Pastor Neely made me wish I knew the right jokes to tell to make my mother laugh like that. I didn't know the right jokes, but maybe if I watched her hands as she sliced the peaches, counted how many times she stirred, and learned to gauge by smell the exact moment to take the cobbler from the oven—maybe I could make a cobbler that pleased God. And maybe that would please my mother.

On those Mondays that God didn't come, my mother would toss the cobbler in the garbage after dinner, pour herself a large tumbler of Tanqueray, and send me to bed early. Sometimes he wouldn't come for several weeks in a row. Or several months. I remembered one time a toothless old woman testified at church saying, "God may not come when you want him, but he's always right on time."

One Monday night, when I was eight, I lay in bed, restless, thinking about that cobbler in the bottom of the garbage can. But this night, I remembered that I had taken the garbage out and put in a fresh bag right before my mother threw the cobbler away. I got up, as if I had to go to the bathroom, but I went into the kitchen instead.

In the darkness, I reached down into the garbage can until my fingertips were wet and sticky. I grabbed a handful of the cobbler and shoved it all in my mouth at once. The sugary juice dribbled over the corner of my mouth down to my chin as I chewed. I savored the peaches and the soft bits of crust soaked through with the syrup. Nothing had ever tasted so good. From memory, I pictured every movement of my mother's hands. How she dunked the peaches in boiling water, then ran them under cold tap water to slide the peels off. The easy way she wielded the knife to slice the peaches. The care she took to drain canned peaches when Georgia peaches were out of season.

I wanted to be those peaches. I longed to be handled by caring hands. And if I couldn't, I wanted the next best thing: to make something so wonderful with my own hands.

"What are you doing?"

I swung around. My mother stood in the doorway with her bare arms folded. She wore a faded cotton nightgown that had been sky blue once upon a time.

"I asked you a question," she said, her voice still thick with gin.

Tears streaked my cheeks, and my sticky fingers were still in my mouth. I bit down on them, not sure how to answer her, and afraid not to answer. My mother didn't whup me often—by then, I had learned how to stay on the right side of her anger most of the time. But when she did, it was like she had lowered her bucket into an ancient well of fury that ran far deeper than my present crime. She would wail along with me as she hit me, saying over and over that I had to learn. I had to.

"Answer me."

"I wanted some of the cobbler."

"Is it yours?"

"No, ma'am."

"What did I tell you about taking things that are not yours?"

"It's stealing."

"Who does that cobbler belong to?"

My mother and I had never spoken about what happened on Mondays, but instinct had told me it wasn't something she wanted to talk about, and as a general rule, my mother had no patience for my questions.

"It belongs to . . . to God."

My mother's eyes widened. "Are you sassing me, girl?" She stepped toward me. I ran to the back door and pressed my back against it. Outside, I decided, was still scarier than inside.

My words came tumbling out. "No, Mama. I'm not sassing you. You make the cobbler for God."

"I make the . . . ?" Mama dropped into a chair at the kitchen table. "You think that . . ." She made a sound, something like laughing and coughing and choking all at once.

"Sit down."

I sat in the chair across from her. "I know you don't understand why some things are the way they are," Mama said. "You just haven't lived long enough to know. But *I* know. I know what's best. I know what's good for you."

Mama reached over and touched the back of my hand. The thrill of her touch made me forget for a moment that I was in trouble.

"One thing you gotta understand, though: Pastor Neely is not God," she said. "He is a friend of mine. That's why he comes by here." She spoke with a softness that matched her touch and tamped down my fear. Even when she continued, saying "But that ain't nobody's business but mine," some of the softness remained. I wished this softer mama would show up more often.

"Do you understand me?"

I didn't. Not completely. But I understood enough to know I was being asked to keep a secret. "Yes, ma'am," I said.

And it was an easy secret to keep. First there were the questions of who I would tell and why they would care to know. Not being allowed to spend time with my classmates outside of school had positioned me firmly on the sidelines of any group of girls that would have had me in the first place. Pretty much everybody on our side of town was poor. But thanks to my too-small or too-large Goodwill clothes and run-over shoes, the other girls never found themselves last in the elementary school pecking order.

And while those girls (save Latasha Wilson) weren't much better off than me, at least their hair was brushed into carefully parted, well-oiled ponytails with barrettes most days. This currency of being neat and cared for was always out of my reach, a fact that was evident every time I stood on a chair in front of the bathroom mirror, struggling to wrestle my giant ball of thick hair into a single puff atop my head. Mama always said she had never been good at that kind of thing—she had loose curls that didn't require taming—and she was relieved when I could finally do it myself.

So I had no real friends to confide in about Pastor Neely, and the idea of saying anything at all—not to mention my mother's business—at length to an adult? The idea of it made my stomach flip-flop.

Even if my mother hadn't asked me to keep her secret, what happened one Monday when I was ten guaranteed I would never tell.

One hot day in late May, I was walking home from the bus stop. Our electricity had been shut off again, and all the windows in our house were open, to catch a breeze. As I approached the house, one of those wished-for breezes swept past, lifted the curtains at our bedroom window and held them in mid-air long enough for me to see Pastor Neely's huge, bare ass, to see him standing and thrusting against my mother, crushing her against our dresser.

As I walked closer toward the front door, the curtains continued their air dance, and I could see more of Pastor Neely. I could see him gripping my mother's hips with those fat sausage fingers of his covered, I imagined, with sticky syrup from the cobbler, oozing down my mother's body, and

I hated him. This was sex, the *it* girls at school giggled about behind their hands.

I got my first period a week later, a shock to both my mother and me. I didn't know what was happening, and at first my mother would only say, "You're too young, you're too young . . ." Her crumpled face and the bulky pad between my legs felt like a punishment.

By the time I turned eleven, I was covered in pimples and wore a 36D bra. My mother was more embarrassed by my breasts than I was, always chastising me to cover up, as if that was possible. I sensed her retreating even further away from me, so I made the first move. I moved out of our bedroom, took over the living room, and slept on the couch.

When I stopped going to church, my mother didn't push.

Even though I no longer ate the peach cobblers out of the garbage can at night, my hunger remained. I still watched my mother make them because I didn't want to forget how she did it. Maybe I could make one for myself. Once I asked if she could buy extra peaches so that I could make a cobbler. "I don't have money to waste on you messing around in my kitchen" was her answer.

At fourteen, I got a job at the mall, at Thom McAn shoe store. I would buy my own damned peaches.

I made my cobblers on Friday nights when

my mother would hole up in her bedroom with a bottle of Tanqueray and I had the kitchen to myself. I didn't change a single step or ingredient, so my cobblers tasted as good as my mother's, even better eaten off a plate instead of my fingers. I ate cobbler with every meal throughout the weekend until it was all gone. I would soak the empty pan in the sink, my hands lingering in the warm dishwater. I had made something wonderful.

Only once did my mother acknowledge my cobbler making. She came out of her room one Friday night and stood in the doorway of the kitchen wearing an oversized flannel shirt, gin in hand, watching me. The liquor made her slower and more deliberate, softer, and even more beautiful somehow. Her hair was out of its usual bun, and it flowed over her shoulders. She was in her mid-thirties, but looked girlish, like a life-sized doll.

"You think you know what you doin', huh? Think you so smart. Smarter than everybody."

I turned away and went back to stirring the batter for my crust.

My mother walked over to me, so close I could smell the gin on her breath. "There's book smart, and there's *life* smart," she said. "If you was life smart, you wouldn't try and be anything like me."

I imagined asking Pastor Neely to try my cobbler. But besides our awkward hellos, we never said a word to each other. If I was in the kitchen when he arrived, I would leave and go into the living room. Still, I imagined him tasting my cobbler and telling me it was better than my mother's—the best in the world. I also imagined serving him a piece with ground-up glass baked into the crust and watching him crumple to the floor. More than that, I wanted my mother to know and be proud that I could make a good cobbler. Mostly I just wanted my mother.

By eleventh grade, I had tired of fighting off boys and gave in. But none of the boys I fooled around with in the park behind the school deserved my peach cobbler. Mostly they just wanted to mess with my breasts, and mostly I just wanted to be touched.

One Monday night, in mid-January of my junior year, my mother came into the living room with me after Pastor Neely left. I felt my chest tighten. I much preferred our usual routine where I couldn't bear to look at her after he left and she didn't seem to want my company either. But that night, she joined me on the couch and handed me a piece of paper.

"This is the Neelys' address. They are expecting you Tuesdays right after school. For tutoring. Trevor is having trouble in math," she said. "I told him how you get straight As and all in the advanced classes. He's just going to tell her that the school recommended you as a tutor."

He. And *her*. So we were not going to say Pastor Neely's name or his wife's name.

Of course, there were many things we were not going to say.

I was going to keep my mouth shut, as expected. As it was always expected.

That first Tuesday, when First Lady Neely threw open the front door of their McMansion before I could even knock, I realized that she was black, not white. Up close I could see her full lips and broad nose. And looking at her relaxed hair pulled back into a loose ponytail, I could tell it was almost time for a touch-up.

"Hello, Olivia! I'm Marilyn Neely," she said, ushering me into the foyer. "But you can call me Miz Marilyn. And I hope you don't mind," she said, wrapping her bony arms around me. "I'm a hugger!"

Realizing that she wasn't the white woman ice queen I remembered from years ago made me feel even worse about being in her home. I willed myself not to stiffen at her touch, tried to remember that I hadn't done anything wrong, that I wasn't the one betraying her. I touched her back lightly during the hug, and I could feel her shoulder blades protruding. I felt huge by comparison, like I could crush her bones with one hard squeeze. With one hard truth.

I felt light-headed at the image of such power,

at the memory of Pastor Neely's naked ass, and at the thought of my mother. *What if this woman can read my thoughts?* I swayed and almost lost my balance.

"Are you okay, honey?" Miz Marilyn held me by my shoulders with a surprisingly strong grip. On each of her hands, three huge diamond rings sparkled.

She guided me to a small sofa inside the foyer. "This settee has been in my family for fifty years," she said. "My papa used to say *settee* was French for 'useless chair'!"

She laughed at her own joke, and I tried to smile, but my lips, like the rest of me, were shaking. "I'm fine," I said. "Just a little weak. I skipped lunch today." Which wasn't a complete lie. I skipped lunch most days because cafeteria food was gross and I preferred the company of books over that of my peers.

Miz Marilyn clapped her hands. "Well, come on into the dining room. I have a nice snack prepared, and that is where you and Trevor will be working. *Trevor!*" she yelled up the stairs.

Trevor Neely was a star football player and college-bound senior at Woodbury Academy, a local private school. He was fair, tall, and lean like his mother. No doubt he had his pick of girls at school. I thought he would have a problem with his tutor being a year younger than him, and a girl. But if either of those things bothered him, he never said.

After his mother introduced us and then left, closing the pocket doors of the dining room behind her, Trevor stared openly at my breasts. His gray eyes flashed with confidence.

I picked up a finger sandwich, chicken salad, from the tray Miz Marilyn had prepared. Between bites, I said, "So . . . why don't you show me what you're working on in precalc?"

But Trevor kept staring, at my breasts, into my eyes, then back to my breasts.

"Yes," I told him. "I have big tits. Huge boobs. Giant hooters. Enormous knockers. And yes, you're cute, but your eyes don't work on me. Now cut the bullshit, and let's get to work."

Trevor laughed, showing his perfect teeth. "You all right," he said. "You all right."

He showed me his last test, on which he'd gotten a 69 percent. We went over his mistakes for about half an hour, then he asked to take a break. We ate sandwiches and sipped Coke. This time when Trevor looked at me, I found myself looking away. He really was cute.

"Have you seen that new Fat Boys video? With the Beach Boys?"

" 'Wipeout'?"

"Yeah, that's it. It's a trip," he said, laughing.

"I heard the song on the radio, but I haven't seen the video."

"What? They play it, like, fifty times a day on MTV."

"I don't have cable."

"You don't have cable?"

I shrugged.

"But I know you watch *The Cosby Show*."

"Yep. You know who I can't stand? Vanessa. She is so annoying!"

"She makes me glad I don't have any brothers or sisters."

"Me too. Though I wouldn't mind Denise. She's cool."

"That honey is *foine*. I wouldn't want her for a sister, though. That's illegal!"

We both cracked up, and then silence followed. My hand rested near Trevor's on the dining room table. His fingers were not stubby sausages like his father's. They were long and slim, and I wondered how they would feel inside me, how he would feel inside me. What if I went all the way with him? Something I hadn't done before. I pictured it: Trevor and me, naked and all tangled up, groping and sucking, on the dining room table beneath his mother's crystal chandelier. I felt sick again at the thought, this time at the pit of my stomach. *Sick with desire*. The words took shape in my mind, black and slick like oil, rising from the page of a trashy novel I'd gotten from the grocery store the week before.

In that moment, I understood how enough

desire could drown you, take you all the way under.

I closed my eyes, cleared the fantasies, and pulled myself back to the surface.

At home that night, I took the envelope of money Miz Marilyn had given me and dropped it on the kitchen counter next to where my mother stood washing dishes. I headed for the living room.

"How was it?" my mother called after me.

I stopped without turning around to face her. *How was it? How was it?* Was she serious? *Oh, it was about what you would expect from spending time with the wife and son of the preacher your mom is fucking on a weekly basis.*

"Fine," I said, my back still turned.

"That's it? Just 'fine'?"

"Yes, ma'am."

"Here. Take this. It's yours."

I turned around. My mother held the envelope out to me.

"No, ma'am. I don't want it."

"*Here,*" she said. She shook the envelope. I sighed and took it.

"Sit down." I sat at the table, and my mother sat across from me. "Tell me about the house."

"It's . . . big. And . . . full of old, expensive furniture."

My mother frowned. "What else? What about her?"

"What about her?"

"Watch your tone. And don't get smart with me."

"I'm not. I just . . . I don't know what you want me to say." I shrugged. I felt a strange sense of loyalty to Miz Marilyn and to Trevor. None of us asked to be in this situation.

"She was nice."

"And . . . ?"

"And . . . I don't know. She's not white."

"You thought she was white?" My mother laughed, loud and throaty. "No, she's just high yellow. As black as he is, he likes a high-yellow woman, of course." My mother was only a shade or two darker than Miz Marilyn. I was darker than my mother, but not as dark as Pastor Neely. A sick feeling came over me, for the third time that day: could Pastor Neely be my father? My mother only ever said he was someone I wouldn't want to know.

As if she'd read my mind, my mother said, "Just like your daddy. Black as midnight, but chased high-yellow and white women nonstop."

"May I be excused?"

My mother looked disappointed. "I made you a TV dinner."

"Thanks, but I'm not hungry."

"Did you eat over there?"

"Just some sandwiches."

"What kind?"

I had to bite my tongue. I couldn't believe she was giving the third degree about a damn sandwich. I just wanted to go take a shower. "Chicken salad."

"And what else?"

"Coke."

"And that's it? Hmph."

"Yes, that was it," I said. "May I please be excused?"

My mother waved me away.

Later that night and many nights after over the months I tutored Trevor, I drifted in and out of dreams about him. I had liked a couple of the boys I'd fooled around with, had liked a few others from a distance. But Trevor was the first boy I really crushed on. His big, curious eyes; the round tip of his nose; and his full lips. A smile or a laugh was never far from his mouth. I wanted to kiss him. Every Tuesday brought a new opportunity to kiss him. The way I would catch him looking at me, I was sure the feeling was mutual. But all I allowed myself to do was inhale the sweet mix of hair grease, soap, and sweat emanating from him when our heads hovered together over his precalculus textbook. On the rare occasions when I did allow our eyes to meet for longer than a second, Trevor would smile, satisfied. And I would be flooded with a mix of desire and irrational guilt. Trevor couldn't blame me for what my mother and his father were doing. And while I certainly wasn't going to tell him, my knowing and his not knowing just felt wrong somehow. But what could I do?

All of this cemented my understanding of God as a twisted puppet master watching his creations bounce around, trapped and tangled up in tragedies for his amusement.

Despite the tension, Trevor and I always got back to the work, back to the reason for my being there: he wanted to do well in precalculus, and I wanted him to do well so that he would graduate and I could stop hugging his mother every week, like a Judas by proxy, and frustrating my mother with reports of turkey sandwiches, sloppy joes, and corn dogs. But I would miss spending time with him, guilt and all.

I managed to avoid Pastor Neely for four Tuesdays of tutoring. But on the fifth Tuesday, he opened the door when I rang the bell. I took a step back. My mouth went dry, and I did not return his hello.

Pastor Neely grinned and extended his hand to me the way he did to parishioners during the love offering. I looked down at those fat sausage fingers, and my stomach lurched. He dropped his hand and his grin, but his voice was cheerful. "Come on in. Olivia . . . is it?"

"Yes, sir."

I stepped partway into the foyer, but kept one foot close to the door, imagining the fallout if I just turned and ran.

Trevor came bounding down the stairs. He froze on the last stair and narrowed his eyes at his father. "Where's Mom?"

"She went to check on your Aunt Catherine. She hasn't been feeling well lately."

"Oh," Trevor said. He didn't move from that bottom stair.

"Well, just do whatever you do when your mother is here," Pastor Neely told Trevor. "I'll be downstairs in the study."

Trevor waited until his father was gone before stepping down into the foyer.

"Come all the way in," he said. "You look like you ready to bolt. You okay?"

"Yeah," I said. "Why wouldn't I be?"

"Sometimes people are intimidated by my dad. You look scared."

I managed a laugh I hoped was convincing. "Me? Scared? Please. *You* looked scared."

Trevor's face reddened a bit, and he looked at the ground. "I was just surprised to see him home this early. That's all."

I wasn't buying it. But then he flashed me a smile, so I dropped it.

Miz Marilyn had left us grilled cheese sandwiches wrapped in foil on the dining room table.

Trevor took a huge bite out of a sandwich.

"My mom's not the greatest cook in the world, but she makes a good grilled cheese."

I took a bite. The sandwich was buttery and delicious. "This is goo—," I started to say, but Trevor was on me, his lips on mine, his body pressing mine against the table.

I swallowed the bits of sandwich in my mouth and then returned Trevor's kiss. He slid his hands beneath my shirt and cupped my breasts. I moaned and placed my palm on the table to steady myself.

Trevor reached around to unhook my bra. "No!" I whispered. "We can't. Your dad . . ."

". . . is in his study."

"Yeah, but . . ."

Trevor held his hands up and backed away. "You're probably right."

I exhaled, relieved that he wasn't upset, but also screaming with joy inside, already replaying the kiss in my mind.

"Now you expect me to just sit here with blue balls and solve some polynomial equations," Trevor said. He made a big show of walking wide-legged to his chair.

"You are so silly," I said.

And after that, we started each tutoring session with a brief make-out session. We knew that if Miz Marilyn was going to check on us, it wouldn't be in the first few minutes. Oddly enough, making out with Trevor made me feel less guilty where he and Miz Marilyn were concerned. For a few moments at least, I could forget about our parents, and just be a girl kissing a boy she liked. Simple.

At the end of April, Miz Marilyn turned sixty. "It's my birthday!" she announced as she threw the door open to let me in.

"Happy birthday!" I said.

"I am sixty years old today. No spring chicken!" she chuckled. "You know, Trevor was my miracle child, my change-of-life baby . . ." Trevor had come into the foyer, but turned on his heel when he heard the topic of conversation. Miz Marilyn reached out and pulled him back.

"I thought it wasn't God's will for me to ever be a mother, but he gave me my beautiful boy when I was forty-three!" she said, throwing her arms around Trevor.

"Ma, come on, cut it out," Trevor said, squirming away. "I need to study."

"All right, all right," Miz Marilyn said. "I'll leave you two *scholars* to your work."

In the dining room, Trevor tried to kiss me. "No!" I hissed and pushed him away. I turned my back to him to wipe away tears.

"Okay . . ." he said. "That time of the month, I guess."

"You're not funny."

Trevor shook his head. We sat down and went

over the problems he missed on a pop quiz. Then he started his homework, stopping to ask questions when he needed to. After a while, I started to pack up and leave.

"What are you doing?" Trevor looked at his watch. "We've still got fifteen minutes left."

"So you're a timekeeper now?" I snapped.

"No, I just . . ." Trevor looked dejected. "I just had a question about number six."

I sighed, dropped my bag, and sat back down in the chair. "Look," I said. "If your mother wants to hug you, let her. Don't be an asshole."

The following week, Trevor answered the door when I arrived. He wore a Public Enemy T-shirt and a pair of basketball shorts. Message: *I'm a jock, and I'm righteous*. How could I possibly stay mad at him?

I stepped inside. "Where's Miz Marilyn?"

"She and my dad just left to go the hospital. My aunt's really sick." His voice cracked a little, and he pretended to cough to cover it up.

"I'm sorry. I hope she's okay."

"Yeah," Trevor said. "I heard my mom say she might not make it. Her heart is failing. They are going to make a prayer circle around her. Like that's going to help."

"You don't believe in prayer?"

Trevor looked at me. "I'm a PK. Of course I believe in prayer." His voice dripped with sarcasm.

"What's a PK?"

"Preacher's Kid. I thought everybody knew that."

"Well, you thought wrong."

We stood there, staring at each other.

"I never told anybody," I said, "but I don't believe in prayer either."

Trevor did that half-smile thing and shook his head. "I bet you have a lot of secrets."

"I'm good at keeping secrets."

Trevor reached for my hand, and I gave it to him.

Upstairs in his bedroom, Trevor put a cassette in his boom box and pressed Play. As Keith Sweat crooned "Make It Last Forever," we kissed and undressed each other.

"Wow," Trevor said once my bra and panties were off. Instantly his hands were everywhere. For once I didn't feel embarrassed or annoyed. I felt powerful.

I pushed Trevor back on the bed and straddled him, letting my breasts sweep against his face.

"You ever did it before?" he asked.

"No. You?"

He hesitated a beat too long, so I knew that no matter what he said, the truth was that he hadn't.

He told the truth. And then together we figured out how to put on the condom.

Trevor closed his eyes as he positioned himself between my legs. I wondered what he was thinking about. I was trying not to think about his father and my mother. The white-hot pain of him entering me brought me to tears. Tears from the fresh pain and from old hurts ran together.

"You want me to stop?" Trevor asked, still thrusting.

I never wanted him to stop.

When it was over, we finished the risky business of removing the condom. My fears of getting pregnant, all the what-ifs I had held at bay while we were doing it, they all came flooding back. My mother would kill me. And Miz Marilyn . . . I didn't even want to think about how upset and disappointed she would be. If Trevor was thinking about any of this, he didn't show it. He just adjusted the pillow beneath our heads, laid back, and smiled at me.

I propped myself up on one elbow. "Don't you think we should go back downstairs? Your parents could come back at any time."

"They'll be praying for hours. Trust me."

So I laid down on the pillow next to him and stared at the ceiling. "Now what?"

"You didn't like it?"

"No, it's not that . . . I don't know. It's weird. How something can feel right and wrong at the same time."

"My father would say that what we just did is plain wrong, a sin. Fornication."

"Do you believe that?"

He shrugged.

"Do you believe in God?"

He shrugged again.

"For a long time," I said, "I thought your father was God."

"Yeah. You and me both."

And then Trevor reached for me with one hand and for a condom with the other.

Miz Marilyn's sister died a few days later. When I showed up for Trevor's next tutoring session, I brought Miz Marilyn a peach cobbler I'd baked. I had hoped that Pastor Neely wouldn't be there and was relieved when he wasn't. It would be the last tutoring session; Trevor had finals, then graduation, and then he was off to Morehouse in Atlanta.

"I'm so sorry about your sister," I said.

"Thank you, dear," Miz Marilyn said. "She's at peace now."

Miz Marilyn's eyes were red from crying. It was the first time I'd seen her without a full face of makeup, and her hair was loose and a bit bushy. But she clapped her hands when I showed her the cobbler. "Oh, my word! It almost looks too good to eat. Almost! *Trevor*!"

As Miz Marilyn chattered on about the cobbler and how her sister used to make good apple cobblers, "God rest her soul," I noticed a new framed picture on the hall table. In it, Trevor wore a tux, and his arm was around a pretty light-skinned girl in a seafoam-green prom gown. Her makeup was flawless and her hair was done up in glossy ringlets. They looked like wedding cake toppers, posed and stiff.

"—my best china and silverware. Because a special treat calls for special dishes. Oh, didn't Trevor and Monica look lovely?" Miz Marilyn asked when she saw me staring at the photo. "They took that picture in her backyard. The Caldwells have a beautiful home up in Hillcrest. A perfect backdrop."

A Woodbury Academy girl from Hillcrest. Whose mother hadn't been fucking his father for over a decade.

"Yes," I said. "It's perfect."

In the dining room, I could barely swallow a bite, but Miz Marilyn and Trevor dug into the cobbler. They both said it was the best they'd ever had. Miz Marilyn closed her eyes every time she took a bite. I tried to absorb all this goodness, but I didn't deserve it. I didn't even belong there, sullying her spotless home. Trevor finished his first helping, pushed his plate aside, and ate directly from the pan. I wanted to stab him with my fork.

Trevor kept stealing glances, asking me questions with his eyes. When Miz Marilyn left us alone to study, he stopped me when I asked to see his homework. "You okay?"

"It's not your concern."

"Whoa. You pregnant?"

"What? No!" I said, way too loudly.

"Then what—"

"Nothing. Let's just go over your homework."

"You're not going to tell me what's the matter?"

What was the matter? What was I expecting? For him to take me to the prom just because we'd had sex? He hadn't told me he had a girlfriend, but I also hadn't asked. What did he owe me? What did anyone owe me?

"I didn't know you had a girlfriend."

"Oh," Trevor said. "Yeah."

Yeah? That was it? Yeah?

The next forty minutes felt like a year. Trevor finished his homework. I checked it, and we went over the ones he missed. I spoke as little as possible. My voice was slow and heavy and felt like it belonged to someone else.

When the session was over, I grabbed my bag to leave.

"Wait," Trevor said. He stood up and pulled me to him.

"Let me go." I pushed him away.

Trevor shrugged. "All right. If that's how you want to be."

How did I want to be?

I wanted to be free of other people's secrets.

"Yeah," I said. "That's how I want to be."

In the foyer, Miz Marilyn handed me my cleaned baking pan and my last pay envelope. "With a bonus!" she said, hugging me. As I stepped outside, she called after me. “Please come and see me, anytime. This big old house will be lonely come fall.”

“Yes, ma’am,” I said, knowing I never would.

As soon as I was on the street and out of sight, I ran. I ran and cried the entire bus ride home.

I stormed into the house and found my mother in the kitchen, putting away groceries.

“How was—?”

“Take it!” I threw the envelope at her chest. She put up her hands to block it, and the envelope fell at her feet. I dropped the empty cobbler pan and kicked it across the room as hard as I could. It slammed into the bottom of the stove.

“Girl, I don’t know what’s gotten into you, but—”

“I don’t want his money, and I don’t want him in this house ever again!”

My mother’s laugh was dry and scornful. She crossed the room and got right up in my face. “Whose money do you think keeps us in this house? When was the last time you remember the lights being shut off? Or the water? You can’t, can you? Instead of talking about what you don’t want, you need to be thanking him.”

I shook my head. “No. I won’t ever thank him for cheating on his wife, for bringing me around his family,” I said. “And I would have rather been homeless, but I guess I should thank you for fucking him all these years to keep a roof over my head.”

My mother raised her hand and slapped me so hard across the mouth, I almost lost my footing. I raised my hand to slap her back, and she looked up at it. "Go ahead," she said. "Take your best shot. And then get the hell out of my house."

I balled my hand into a fist. "Why couldn't you leave me out of this?" Tears streamed down my face. My mother kept her eyes on my raised fist. "Look at me!" I screamed. But she wouldn't.

"You could've said no," my mother whispered.

"Could I, really? I don't recall being asked. So don't you try and turn this on me!"

My mother slapped me again. "You watch your mouth!"

I raised my fist again. "I hope Pastor Neely chokes and dies on the next cobbler you make."

"Don't talk like that, Olivia! God don't like ugly."

"There's nothing you can say to me about God. Ever. Because you're the ugliest. You and Pastor Neely. The ugliest." My chest was heaving, and I couldn't stop the tears even if I had wanted to. "So you don't have to worry anymore, Mama," I said, "about me wanting to be anything like you. I swear, my life won't be anything like yours. Because it will be sweet, and it won't be crumbs."

And then I dropped my fist. Because in the meantime, I had nowhere to go.

SNOWFALL

—

BLACK WOMEN *aren't meant to shovel snow.* Rhonda mumbles this as we are knee-deep in the stuff. We have to do it. When it snows heavily overnight, we wake before the sun comes up to get dressed, shovel ourselves out, clear off our Honda, prevent slip-and-fall lawsuits from neighbors, and still get to work on time.

But I know where Rhonda is coming from. We, who apparently are built for everything, are simply not built for this. No gloves exist that keep our hands from freezing as we move snow and ice from one spot to another and from the car windshield. No boots exist that can keep the cold from numbing our toes. No number of layers and waterproof pants keep the chill at bay. We feel it through our chests. And no, the physical activity does not warm us up. It makes us resentful.

We don't like to admit it, but the snow is beautiful. When it's that light dusting that rests on bare branches, when it looks all puffy and cottony and innocent. The problem is the work snow demands.

Still, I say, "Maybe it's just us," as I clear a stripe into the snow on the trunk of the car. "All the Black women born and raised in this city . . . well, yeah, there aren't *that* many . . . but they must be used to it by now. It's only our first winter here. Maybe in time . . ."

"Not everything has to be interrogated, Arletha," Rhonda says as she scrapes away at a patch of ice on the edge of the driveway. I'm Arletha when she's pissed at me; I'm Leelee the rest of the time, which is most of the time. Most of the time we live in the space between my need to dissect and her need to keep things whole with declarative statements.

Right now we are living in the space of the morning after yet another bedtime conversation that started innocently enough. We are living in the space of me staring at the ceiling for hours, then oversleeping, again; of Rhonda having to do the bulk of the snow and ice clearing, again. The third time I rolled over and asked Rhonda to give me five more minutes, she didn't answer. By the time I woke up, I could hear her shovel stabbing the sheet of ice on the driveway. Through our bedroom window, I watched her work. Skullcap pulled down tight over her locs which fell over her shoulders and were dotted with snowflakes. Slim arms delivering harder blows to the ice than seemed possible.

I brush the last mounds of snow off the hood of the car and return my scraper to the trunk. Rhonda is almost done clearing the ice.

When my teaching job at the university brought us here last summer, we knew there would be snow, but we didn't know the stuff would shape the course of so many of our days and nights. Neither of us has fully mastered driving in the snow yet, and our experience with Uber drivers has been hit or miss. So we stock up on groceries and run as many errands as possible on clear days.

But it's not just the snow. The cold temperatures alone have kept us in binge-watching episodes of *The Office* and having Thai food delivered. There's just something about being out in it that makes us mildly cranky and singularly focused on getting to the next heated place.

We were born and raised in warmer places, Georgia and Florida. Warmer too in the residual charm, polite smiles, and gentility of the white people whose ancestors owned ours. In the South, the weather does not force tears from your eyes, causing the faces of passing strangers to register worry about you, for a millisecond. It's the wind, you want to tell them, but a millisecond is not enough time. In the South, the weather does not hurt you down to your bones or force you to wake up a half an hour early to remedy what has been done to your steps, your sidewalk, your driveway, and your car as you slept.

But the South has hurricanes, they say. Yes, but not damn-near daily, not for a full quarter of the year.

You tell people up here that you're from the South, and nine times out of ten, they say the same old thing: "I'm sure you miss the sunshine." Rhonda and I both miss taking sunshine and easy morning commutes for granted. But what we really miss are the laughter and embrace of our mothers and grandmothers and aunties, kin and not kin. We miss the big oak tables in their dining rooms where, as kids in the seventies and eighties, we ate bowl after bowl of their banana pudding as they talked to each other about how much weight you'd gained, like you weren't even there. We miss helping them snap green beans and shell peas sitting at their kitchen tables watching *The Young and the Restless* on the TV perched on the pass-through. We miss how they loved Victor Newman, hated Jill Foster, and envied Miss Chancellor and how she dripped diamonds and chandeliers.

We miss their bare brown arms reaching to hang clothes on the line with wooden pins. We miss their sun tea brewed all day in big jars on the picnic table in the backyard, then later loaded with sugar and sipped over plates of their fried chicken in the early evening. We miss lying next to them at night in their four-poster beds with too-soft mattresses covered by ironed sheets and three-generation-old blankets. We miss their housecoats, perfumed with Absorbine Jr. liniment and hints of the White Shoulders they'd spritzed on from an atomizer that morning before church. We miss tracing the soft folds in their skin when we held hands and watched our favorite TV shows in their beds. *Dallas*, *Dynasty*, *Knots Landing*, and *Falcon Crest*.

We miss how they laughed and were easy with each other. How their friendships lasted lifetimes, outlasting wayward husbands and ungrateful children. Outlasted that time Alma caught Joe cheating and she whacked him on the top of the head with the sword he'd brought back from the war, but he told the people at the hospital he didn't know who did it. Outlasted having to hide your medicine bottles in your shoes because, otherwise, seven of your nine children were liable to steal them. We miss how they seemed to judge everyone but themselves. Or maybe that judgment was in the "nerve" pills they procured from the Chinese doctor on Bay St. who didn't ask questions. We miss their furtive cups of brown liquor on Friday and unabashed cries for Jesus come Sunday.

We miss their one gold tooth that made us wonder who they had been as young women.

We miss their blue crabs, the shells boiled to a blood red in wash tubs atop bricks over makeshift fires built in the yard. The wash tubs reminded us of cauldrons, full of rock salt– and cayenne-drenched water bubbling and rolling, mesh bags of seasonings and halved onions and peppers floating on top, along with potatoes and ears of corn. We miss how they stood over those cauldrons like witches, stirring a potion. With sweat beading on the tips of their noses and smoke swirling around their hands and wrists, they wielded long-handled spoons to press the frantic, flailing crabs toward their deaths.

We miss how they made our Easter dresses and pound cakes and a way out of no way.

But we lost all those things when we chose each other. Only the memories remain. Which is why, even though we grew up in different places, so many of our bedtime conversations start with "Remember when . . . ," as we lie there in the dark with our nostalgia and nothing to distract us from it. Not even each other, not anymore.

—

It did snow once in my little town in Florida. In 1989. I was home from college for winter break. I was visiting Tonya, a childhood friend, when my mom called her house looking for me, worried. Had I seen the weather report? I hadn't. When she told me the forecast called for snow and ice, I laughed and asked if she'd been drinking.

Mama huffed. "Girl, I'm serious. This weather ain't to be played with. Mayretta said over by her, cars just slip-sliding all over the road because these people don't know how to drive in it. I know I asked you to stop by Church's on your way home and get me a two-piece, but you just come straight on home now."

"Yes, ma'am."

But of course I didn't listen.

I stayed at Tonya's another hour. Mama told me later that she tried to call back, but apparently Tonya's mother was on the phone and they didn't have call-waiting. And when Mama finally got through, I'd left. Of course this was before cell phones. So the minute I walked in the door, Mama started fussing.

"I was worried sick, thinking you were dead in a ditch somewhere!"

I held out the bag of Church's chicken to her, and she looked at it like it was an alien.

"I told you—"

"I know," I said. "But the roads between Tonya's and Church's and Church's and here were fine. And I know you really wanted the chicken. I got you all wings." I held the bag out to her again. "And I remembered your hot pepper."

My mama dropped down into her favorite armchair and laughed and cried all at once. She pulled me down onto her lap and rocked me. I was as big as she was, so we must've been a sight.

"Leelee, you're all I've got in this world," Mama said. "The idea of anything happening to you . . ."

It had always been just Mama and me. Mama never married or, to my knowledge, dated. My father didn't want to be one, at least not mine. Mama told me he had a wife and kids and was a deacon at the church she and her family used to go to before I was born. She said the Lord had given me to her when she was forty-one—"No spring chicken!"—and He doesn't make mistakes. I knew Mama loved me. I knew she always worked two jobs and sacrificed so I could have everything I needed and most everything I wanted. Disney World when I was five, when it was all she could do to keep the lights on. Sending me ten-dollar money orders at college when my tuition was the same amount she earned in a year at her second job. That's why I'd insisted on bringing her the chicken; she did everything for me and so little for herself.

But like a beautiful quilt in summertime, my mother's love was the suffocating kind, the kind you chafe against and don't miss until the seasons change and it's gone.

Back then, I didn't know if my mother would still love me if she knew that Tonya was more than just a friend. And I wasn't trying to find out.

—

Rhonda and I are not without Black women friends in this city. There's Faith, Staycee, Melanie, Kelli. But friendship is not the same as history, just as a bone is not the same as its marrow. These friends, they tell us that this city—of iron and steel and cold—is better, safer than where we come from. They imagine where we come from and see Confederate flags and rednecks and dusty dudes with gold grillz rapping about bitches and hos. They don't see home.

When we lie in bed at night and "remember when," Rhonda doesn't see home either. Just sepia moments and sepia people, artifacts frozen in amber. Like putting the well-worn photo album back on the shelf, or turning off the TV after watching *Good Times* on TV Land. She drifts off to sleep so easily. Leaving me alone to fend off my thoughts.

Last night, my thoughts won. I stared at the ceiling and thought about my mother lying in her bed, a quilt and a portable heater sufficient for winter in her world. I haven't spoken to her since October, but even then we pretty much just checked in to make sure the other person was alive. We talked about the Ladies Auxiliary fish fry and the hat she bought for Women's Day at church; which elderly neighbor's son got sent to prison, third strike, for selling drugs; whether or not I like my job at the university (yes). And then the usual tension returned and the regret we each felt—for calling, for answering—was palpable.

On these rare calls, my mother never asks about Rhonda. I stared at the ceiling and wondered if my mother still refers to Rhonda as "some girl she met on the internet" when she talks to Miss Mayretta and her other friends about us. She knows Rhonda's name because I told her. I told her everything about me she claimed she didn't know, an ignorance belied by her questions, years of endless questions, about the nameless boys who never called, never took me to prom, never gave her a different reason to be ashamed of me.

My mother knew Rhonda's name and she refused to say it. Refused to meet her. Refused to do anything but pray for my soul. As I walked out her front door for the last time eight months ago, she hurled the words at my back: "Running off from here with some *girl* you met on the internet. Who raised you?"

Leelee, you're all I've got in this world . . .

How could my mother's world just keep right on spinning without me in it?

Maybe it hadn't. Maybe she was lying in bed thinking about me too, worrying. Maybe.

Rhonda's mother had put her out as a teenager. They hadn't spoken in twenty years. Rhonda had couch surfed for a while, turned eighteen, moved to the city, and got a job at the post office. She saved up for an apartment of her own and vowed never again to be anywhere she wasn't wanted. When I met her, we were thirty, and she'd just bought a house. We'd visited back and forth between her town and mine for a few years until I got the job at the university. She didn't hesitate when I asked her to move here with me.

"You are home, LeeLee," she'd said. And at first I didn't catch what she meant. Then I did. When we first moved here, I believed she could be right. I believed that we were all the home either of us could ever need. Through the end of a mild summer, and through a gorgeous red-gold fall, I believed it.

And then last night, after an hour or so of staring at the ceiling, I did something I never do. I woke Rhonda up. And I asked her, "Do you ever think about us moving back South, back home?"

Earlier this year, a cousin had told Rhonda that whenever people asked about her, her mother told them she was probably dead somewhere, even though the cousin had let her know that Rhonda was alive and well.

In the dark, I couldn't make out Rhonda's face, but in the ensuing silence I imagined her blinking her way out of the sleep fog. Then she said, "Arletha, I already told you where home is. For me."

And immediately, I wished I could take the question back.

—

Rhonda leans the shovel against the side of the house and sprinkles salt on the cleared driveway and sidewalk. I wait for her inside the warm car. With only one car and a shitty mass transit system, I will drop her off at her clerk job at the courthouse and then drive to campus. On Fridays, I teach an afternoon class, Black Feminisms, so I have a few hours to get some grading and prep done.

When Rhonda is done with the salt, she climbs in beside me. I brush a smattering of snowflakes from her locs and they melt from the heat of my hand. I can't tell if she stiffened at my touch or if I just imagined it. Her silence as I back out of the driveway suggests the former.

"Forecast says there's another storm coming through later," I say. "How many more weeks of this shit?"

"Whatever that groundhog says, I guess," Rhonda says.

It's slow-going down the steep hills that lead out of our neighborhood. I fear the brakes locking up and us coasting right through a stop sign. A bigger fear is other drivers, probably natives who slow down very little if at all on days like this. Once the roads are clear, it's a free-for-all. But I guess if you've been here long enough, you have more confidence that the black road is just road and not black ice. Rhonda and I don't yet have a critical mass of data points to give us that confidence. But the natives don't know this, of course. They ride our bumper, honk, or swerve around us when we go too slowly for their liking. I want to hang a sign in the back window that says, "We are not from here. Please understand."

Rhonda just says, "Fuck these people," and flips them off as they whiz by us.

But today's ride into the city is fuck-free. Rude drivers pass and honk without a word from Rhonda. In front of the courthouse, I lean over to kiss her before she gets out of the car, and our lips barely touch before she's gone. How long had it been since we'd done anything more in bed than kiss and reminisce?

But the kiss, such as it is, is still a kiss. And I wonder if I will ever stop noticing and cataloging all the things we do here that we didn't—couldn't—do back home. I wonder if that catalog will ever grow long enough to become enough. For me.

Once I get to campus, it's harder than usual to find parking because snow has been plowed into some of the spaces. Eventually I find a spot two blocks from my office on a tree-lined side street. I brace myself for the cold and throw open the car door.

I step out and my feet slide from under me in an instant. My butt slams onto the patch of ice, and my shoulder and back scrape against the base of the car when I land. The car door blocks my view, and my first thought is *Does anyone see me?* But I'm not sure whether I want to be seen.

The cold seeps through my waterproof pants and pain shoots up from my lower back to my shoulders. I want to get up, but I'm afraid of slipping and falling again. I can hear people walking and driving past. I could call out to them. I could get help. I look up at the sky, which is gray like the branches overhead. The branches bend toward me, yielding beneath the weight of the snow piled along them.

A thought crystallizes and takes hold, a thought I haven't had in years, maybe a decade: I want my mother.

If my phone weren't in my purse in the back seat of the car, I would call my mother right this minute. My mother who had been my soft place to land. Until she wasn't.

Everything hurts, and I suspect standing up will hurt even more. I wince at the thought of walking the two blocks to my office. Then I tell myself I'm being ridiculous. *Get up. Get up get up get up.* I repeat this in my head and then under my breath until I am on my knees. I hoist myself back into the driver's seat and slam the door shut. I turn the car on and the heat. I'm sobbing now, and it's as if the sound belongs to someone else. Like the time I woke up from minor surgery annoyed that there was a woman nearby who wouldn't stop crying, not realizing that the woman was me.

It hurts to reach back and grab my purse, but I do it anyway. I take out my phone and pull up my mother's number. I sit there with my finger hovering over the Call button, for forever it seems. But then I scroll through the Recent Calls list and tap Rhonda's name. I try to get the crying under control before she answers, but I can't.

"Leelee, baby, slow down, slow down," she says. "I can't understand what you're saying. What happened?"

"I hate this fucking snow!"

"Okay . . ."

"I hate the snow. I hate winter. I hate this city! I don't want to be here."

Silence. Rhonda sighs. "Where do you want to be?"

"I . . . don't know."

"I think you do know."

"I slipped."

"What?"

"I slipped and fell getting out of the car. I'm fine. But . . . I almost called my mother."

Silence. And then Rhonda says, "Must be nice."

I want to explain how it was just a primal reaction, this urge to call my mother. I want to tell her that she is home too, that she is now my soft place to land, and I am hers.

But nothing I can say will change the fact of my mother-privilege: I could call my mother if I wanted to and she would answer and she might even offer a modicum of comfort and concern, same as she would offer a stranger. I could get that, at least. Rhonda could not.

"LeeLee, if you're sure you're fine," Rhonda says, "I have to get back to work."

Fresh tears sting my eyes. "I'm sure. Yeah."

The call drops, and I return the phone to my purse. I push through the pain and get out of the car again, this time stepping over the icy patch. The walk to the office isn't too bad, but I can feel a bruise pulsing across my back and shoulders.

By the time my class starts, I've taken three Tylenol, and I get through it by sitting in a chair in the front of the room instead of standing and lecturing like I normally do. I feel like maybe I'm moving a beat slower than usual. But my students, an engaged group of twelve women and two men, don't seem to notice. I tell them they are the only bright spot in an otherwise awful day. I'm certain this weirds them out, but I felt like saying it.

Later, when Rhonda gets in the car, she asks how I'm feeling. I tell her I'm fine, and we make the slow crawl through rush-hour traffic.

"LeeLee . . . I'm sorry for what I said earlier. 'Must be nice.' "

"It's okay, babe. I get it."

"Actually, it's not okay. Just because my . . . just because somebody hurt me doesn't make it okay for me to hurt you, to not be there the way you need me to be."

I'm not sure what to say. The snow is just starting to come down hard as we enter our neighborhood. I pull the car into the driveway and push through the pain again to slowly ease out of the car. When my feet are steady, I notice Rhonda standing next to the driver's side door with her car keys in her hand.

"Head on upstairs, and I'll see you in a few," she says.

"Where are you going? It's snowing."

"I know. I'll be all right."

"But where are you going?"

Rhonda shakes her head. "Just go in the house and get yourself in a warm bath. Please?"

I go inside, run the bath, and try not to worry. Our tub is the claw-foot kind, the kind we'd had in my house growing up. Rhonda thinks I chose this house because of the tub, and she might be right. There were houses in better shape and in better neighborhoods than this one, but only this one had a claw-foot tub. I sink down, letting the water cover my back and shoulders, letting my eyelids close.

I guess this is how Rhonda felt the night of the first snow. I was out in it, driving, and she was at home, worried. She had stayed home from work that day to wait for the electrician to come and replace some outlets in the house. Traffic was awful because of the snow and an accident, so by the time I got home, it had been dark for a while. Rhonda had been torn between staying on the phone with me to know I was safe and hanging up so I wouldn't be distracted. Then my phone died and that dilemma was solved.

Now my fully charged phone rests on the floor next to the tub.

I distract myself with a childhood game: I soap up my hands and blow bubbles using my fingers in the "okay" sign position as a makeshift wand. The pain in my back and shoulders begins to subside. I imagine it disappearing into the water mixed in with the soap residue.

Eventually I doze off. I wake up off and on to add hot water and check my phone. At one point, there's a text from Rhonda: *On my way.* I text back *Love you.* No reply.

When I wake up again, Rhonda is standing next to the tub holding one of the oversized T-shirts I sleep in.

"Your back looks like you've been in a fight with a bear . . . and lost. Come on," she says. "I have something for you downstairs." She's changed out of her work clothes and into a strapless sundress I haven't seen since before we moved here. I dry off and follow her downstairs.

I smell it before I see it. The pepper hits my nose first, and then the full array of aromas: onions, peppers, Old Bay, Zatarain's crab boil seasoning.

Grocery store bags litter the floor and counters. The kitchen table is covered in newspapers that Rhonda must've bought at the store. My mother always saved old newspapers to cover the picnic table in the backyard. And just like on my mother's table, there are little bowls of melted butter, a bottle of Louisiana hot sauce, and a pitcher of sweet tea.

On the stove, the stockpot is full of roiling, bright-red water, a tiny, furious ocean full of snow crab legs, potatoes, and ears of corn.

We've tried before to get live blue crabs at Wholey's, the fresh seafood place everyone recommends, but their shipment comes in early Monday mornings and they sell out within minutes.

I turn to Rhonda. She smiles and throws her arms out wide. "They're frozen, but the best cure we got for the winter blues."

Just then, I catch on to the song playing on Rhonda's iPod: "Summertime" by DJ Jazzy Jeff and the Fresh Prince. I two-step my way into Rhonda's arms, and we swing each other around and around the kitchen until the crabs are ready and our faces are damp from the moist, salty air.

Rhonda fills an aluminum pan with crabs and sets it in the middle of the table. I pour us some tea.

"Not that you need my permission," Rhonda says as she joins me at the table, "but it's okay with me if you want to call your mother. I mean, don't let me be the reason you don't call her. And maybe you want to go see her. Spend some time with her. She calls, not much, but that means she is leaving space for you in her life."

I try to detect any trace of resignation or martyrdom beneath her words, but as is always the case, what Rhonda says is exactly what she means.

"Babe," I say, "the space my mother has left for me isn't big enough for two."

Rhonda nods, and we dig in.

Outside, snow blankets our deck. It will fall all night, and tomorrow, we'll again do its bidding.

HOW TO MAKE LOVE TO A PHYSICIST

—

***HOW DO* you make love to a physicist?** You do it on Pi Day—pi is a constant, also irrational—but the groundwork is laid months in advance. First you must meet him in passing at a STEAM conference. As a middle school art teacher, you are there to ensure the A(rts) are truly represented and not lost amid the giants of Science, Technology, Engineering, Math. But as a Black woman, you are there playing Count the Negroes, as you do at every conference. He is number twelve, at a conference of hundreds. On the first day of the conference, you notice him coming down the convention center escalator as you ride up. You try to guess which letter of the acronym he is there to represent. His face and baby dreads give you equal parts "poet" and "high school math teacher."

On the second day of the conference, you see him again at a breakout session, "Arts Integration and Global Citizenry." He's chatting with the presenter—a sista, number thirteen—before the session begins. From what you overhear, you glean that they know each other from their undergrad days in Atlanta in the early nineties. They have a lot of people in common at their respective alma maters. They promise to catch up again before the conference is over. You notice she's wearing a wedding ring, and he is not.

As you're leaving the breakout session, he notices you noticing him. His smile is brilliant; you smile back. He falls in step with you, extends his hand, and introduces himself. He says "Eric Turman," but you hear "Erick Sermon." And your eyes widen and then narrow because you think he's joking, in a weirdly esoteric way.

"No, Eric *Turman*," he says again, laughing. "Not the guy from EPMD."

"Got it," you say. "I'm Lyra James. Not to be confused with Rick James."

Eric chuckles. "But often confused with Lyra, home to one of the brightest stars in the night sky."

The compliment takes you by surprise, and you're probably doing a shitty job of hiding it. "So you're . . . a science teacher?"

He is not a science teacher, nor is he a poet. He's a physicist and chair of the education programs committee for the American Physics Society.

You make small talk about "Arts Integration and Global Citizenry." He asks what brings you to the conference and you tell him you teach middle school art—sculpting, printmaking, painting, fiber arts, ceramics. He asks if you will tell him more over lunch. And you do. And then the conversation continues over dinner—you learn what the chair of the education programs committee for the American Physics Society does—and then in the bar of the conference hotel, over drinks. And then on a sofa in the lobby. You each share your top five MCs. You debate Scarface vs. Rakim for number one.

You notice his thick eyelashes, large hands, and a little scar next to his right eyebrow. When he lifts his newsboy cap a few times to scratch his head, you see the baby dreads are neat and well moisturized.

He tells you about his job, the one that pays the bills, where he develops astrophysics and cosmology theories, and conducts research to test those theories. "I aspire to be an astronaut as a side hustle, but NASA won't return a brotha's calls." He shrugs. "What about you?"

"Me?" you say. "Oh, I just have the one job."

"And your aspirations?"

You take a deep breath and spill your dreams. "You know that school LeBron James started? I want to start one like that. A bunch of them, actually, all over the country. But I'll start with one, serving entire families. That's really the key, you know?"

He knows. And then before you know it, it's after midnight, and you're both still wearing your conference lanyards, and together, you are solving all of public education's problems, but for want of an end to systemic racism, abolishment of the current system of school funding, and a few billion dollars. Eric has pulled out his phone, made a few calculations, recorded the recommendations you've given him—of artists, works of art, books, public school advocacy programs. He is curious and he's listening.

At 2:13 a.m., he says, "Well, you are refreshing." And you feel anything but, because those French 75s you had at the bar have made you drowsy. And because it's 2:13. But you want him to keep talking, to keep listening. *Maybe invite him to come up? No, too soon.* You don't think he's a serial killer; that's not it. It's that you don't want him to think you're that kind of woman. The kind your mother warned you not to be, so you have not been. You are forty-two.

Maybe ask him to meet for breakfast in the morning, then? No, too presumptuous.

Your eyes must've glazed over as you debated yourself, because he says, "I better let you get some rest. I've really enjoyed talking to you."

And you both stand and stretch. But then

you just stand there, looking at each other, not leaving.

"I hope I'm not being too presumptuous," he begins, "but would you like to meet for breakfast?"

How do you make love to a physicist? On the flight home from the conference, you tally all the things you have in common:

- You're tired of people asking why you're still single.
- You care about children, but don't want any of your own.
- Fall is your favorite season.
- You're not a fan of Tyler Perry, and you're tired of people insisting you become one.
- You both have terrible vision and had to navigate your childhood being teased. ("Your glasses so thick, you can see the future" was a perennial favorite.)
- The first Aunt Viv is your favorite.
- In the case of Prince vs. Michael Jackson, you got Prince.

You took all your meals with him for the rest of the conference and talked for hours and hours but left so many things unsaid. Like how you had a high school sweetheart and a college sweetheart and a grad school sweetheart. How men chose you, and you devoted years to the relationships, but never quite felt at home in your body with them—an understanding your therapist has helped you to articulate. You didn't tell him how you stayed until those men decided to leave you for women more at home in their bodies, more sure of themselves, prettier.

You didn't tell him that, as corny and clichéd as it sounds, you're more accustomed to speaking through your art. Paintings and sketches you framed and gave as gifts, or framed and hung in your own house. But these days, you mostly just pour yourself into your students. It's safer that way.

You didn't tell him how, one by one over the decades, you'd lost all your good girlfriends to marriage and motherhood, your friendships reduced to children's birthday parties and the rare Girls' Night Out.

You didn't tell him that aside from the occasional online dating fling, plus some fumbling around with a childhood friend when he's between women he would actually date, you're celibate for months at a time.

Later your therapist will ask why any of those things needed to be said to a man you just met. You know she has a point, but you have no answer other than that maybe you're the kind of woman who should come with a warning, a disclaimer.

If Eric had withheld even a fraction of the things you withheld, that would be a lot of stuff. By the time your plane touches down, you've resolved that you will never know the real him, or if he was even sincere. At baggage claim, you'll decide that it had just been the excitement of the moment, that he'd get back to his life and forget all about you. And you should try to do the same. So you delete his number from your phone.

That night, when you are back home in your own bed, you send your colleagues in the math and science departments a long email detailing your desire to collaborate with them in the coming school year.

How do you make love to a physicist? You take out your charcoal and sketch his face from memory. You tell your therapist about him and how he didn't forget you, but you're allowing his phone calls to go unanswered and leaving his texts on "read." Because you're not good at stuff like this.

"Stuff like what?" your therapist asks.

"Men. It never works out."

"But you've sketched his face. And told me about him. Why?"

"Because we had a great moment. But that's all it was."

"Then why is he still texting you?"

"Just being nice."

She tilts her head in that *Girl, please* way she does right before she challenges you. She asks, "Is this another example of you talking yourself out of potentially good things?"

How do you make love to a physicist? You continue reading his text messages, even though you don't respond to them. He's been texting for weeks, undaunted. He asks how you're doing, tells you how he's doing and what he's doing. He's presented his proposal to his board for an arts and sciences summer camp and family retreat. He thanks you for the inspiration.

One Sunday after church while you are at your mother's for dinner, he texts you a picture of a deep orange and red sunset with the caption, *Best scattering of light rays ever.* You don't realize you're smiling until your mother asks, "Why are you smiling?" She sounds more suspicious than curious. And you wonder when she last saw you smiling, this woman who insists on sending you home every week with enough leftovers for ten people then asks when you're going to lose some weight so you can meet a man.

When you go back to school to set up your classroom for the new year, there is a package from Eric in your box in the faculty mail room. You wonder how he knew where to find you, then you remember the name of your school was printed on your conference lanyard. He has sent you *Overview: A New Perspective of Earth*, a collection of more than two hundred stunning, high-definition satellite photos of Earth that focus on how people have altered the planet. The collection is named for the "overview effect," the sensation of overwhelm, awe, and new perspective astronauts report upon looking down at Earth as a whole. An aerial view of a planned community in suburban Florida is a colorful mosaic. A shot of retired military and government aircraft in the aircraft boneyard at Davis-Monthan Air Force Base resembles a collection of Native American arrowheads. Tulip fields in the Netherlands look like fiber art.

You display the book prominently in your classroom library. You send Eric a text message: *Thank you for the book. It's wonderful.*

Then you respond to his last text, which was about his board approving his summer camp proposal with full funding. *Congratulations on getting funding!* you write. And he replies, *You're welcome! And thank you.*

That night, you read *Overview* cover to cover. And the next night, you start painting again. You stay up late, getting your rhythm back.

The weekend comes, and you call him, because you're really not a fan of texting anyway, and because maybe it's time. He answers right away. He doesn't ask what took you so long. He's happy to hear from you. And you're both breathless.

You talk. About his summer camp proposal, about what you're each making for dinner and what your weekend plans are. You talk about the new Toni Morrison documentary and what she meant to each of you. You talk about loss.

You continue to talk daily, to have virtual dates,

thanks to video calls. And they're better than any real date you've been on. You binge-watch TV shows together, cook together, drink wine, and watch each other do laundry. You talk for days and nights, and nights that turn into mornings.

Sometimes you wake before dawn, and he's still there, his sleeping face filling your phone screen. Then you settle again, your breathing in sync with his, and you drift off.

How do you make love to a physicist? Ask him if he believes in God. Ask him if he thinks it's possible to reconcile science and religion.

"Physics principles support the notion of God because they tell us that you can't create something from nothing," he says. "Something must have created all of this, unless you believe that we have always existed, that there's no big bang, no beginning point to the universe. I don't know what the mechanism is, but it's some higher power. All that energy had to come from somewhere."

"Oh. I assumed you were an atheist."

"Even Einstein wasn't an atheist," he says. "He talked about God all the time. Now, he didn't believe in a god that was concerned with human behavior, which is the church's obsession and the reason it uses guilt and shame to enforce Christianity."

"You don't think God cares how we treat each other and the planet?"

"I think that's the most important thing. But human beings are capable of doing that outside of the purview of the church. I've studied the Bible cover to cover. So much hinges on translation and interpretation. I grew up Catholic, and I love the ritual of it all. But I've come to understand that belief in a personal god is not essential. Not for me."

You ask, "What about heaven?" But what you really want to ask is *What about hell?*

"What about it?"

Heaven—getting into it, avoiding the alternative—is the whole point of living right, isn't it? Your mother speaks longingly of Judgment Day and the final accounting of who's allowed past the pearly gates, certain that God's accounting will mirror hers. "It will be a very small number," she's fond of saying. "Only those who walk the straight and narrow path shall see the face of God."

And you realize that if God were to welcome everyone into heaven, your mother would abandon Christianity immediately.

You don't know how to answer Eric's question about heaven without sounding like you're quoting a fairy tale about good and evil, reward and punishment.

You take a moment to soak it all in. You think of your mother and the small version of God she clings to, the only version you've ever known and the one you're afraid to let go of. Then you think of how your daily calls with Eric are a kind of ritual, and how when you finally meet up again, it could be a kind of consecration. You are thrilled and terrified at the prospect. Terrified because all you've ever known of religion is that it demands more than you can ever give.

"I guess a person could have heaven right here on earth," you say.

"I do," Eric says. "Every time I see you smile, or hear you talk about your students. And even when you're quiet and painting or just . . . folding towels."

"Heaven is me folding towels?"

"Okay . . . maybe it's you folding fitted sheets. Miracles abound."

How do you make love to a physicist? You invite him to visit in the spring for your first solo art show at a local gallery. It will be a collection of colorful abstract paintings influenced by your reading of *Overview*, Rumi, and the Qur'an, and your rereading of Morrison's *Song of Solomon*. You title the show *Whatever I Say about Love*, a line from Rumi's *The Masnavi*. You're painting now more than you ever have.

The show is still three months away, and already you're imagining your mother wandering around the gallery muttering under her breath, "What is that supposed to be?" the way she did when you lived at home and she'd barge into your bedroom/studio unannounced. You never gave her your framed work as a gift. You stuck with perfume and jewelry.

You ask your therapist if it would be wrong not to invite your mother to the show. She answers your question with a question: "Do you want her there?"

"If I'm honest, the answer is no."

"Then don't invite her."

You're silent, and after a moment, she asks, "How do you feel when you hear me say that?"

"Frightened."

"What are you afraid of?"

"Everything."

How do you make love to a physicist? You start to have sex dreams about him, very, very detailed sex dreams. For the first time in your life, you crave sex. For the first time, you are curious about a man's body, about how you will feel above and beneath him.

But then you remember the sex you've had, and how you had to disappear into yourself to endure it. How you thought about your stomach and your thighs the whole time, wishing you were someone else, imagining he was wishing the same. How sex, for you, was just a way to be touched, a means to an end. How all you ever really wanted was to be touched. But men always want more.

Eric, like any man, would eventually want

more, more than you could give. And he would be disappointed, probably disgusted, with you for leading him on.

So you do one of the hardest things you've ever had to do: you delete his number from your phone again, but this time, you also block it.

How do you make love to a physicist? Forget your home training. Ditch the girdles your mother taught you to wear to harness your belly, your butt, your thighs, your freedom. God forbid something jiggle. God forbid you are soft and unbridled.

Sleep naked.

This is all your therapist's idea. At first you're skeptical and resistant. But when she asks you to just humor her, because what's the downside, you can't think of one.

You take long, hot, soapy showers, catching the water in your mouth until it spills out the corners. You rinse, step out, and rub lavender oil into your still-damp skin, from your scalp to the bottoms of your feet. It's winter, so you bundle up beneath blankets and explore. Use your hands to study the contours and curves of your body, your topography. To study them as fact, without judgment. Pleasure yourself, but slowly, to savor and discover. Every morning and every night.

On the weekends, you sleep in, then wake up and cook hearty comfort meals from scratch—no boxes, no cans, no fast food. Crab and kale omelets, roasted red potatoes, seafood linguini, ginger turmeric butternut squash soup, caramelized Brussels sprouts, roasted beet salad with goat cheese, coconut curries, beef Wellington.

You cook and paint and nap and stroke yourself to sleep at night.

And as your body begins to feel like a home, your courage grows. It grows bigger than your mother's chastisement in the parking lot after service the first time you go to church unbound. She asks why you aren't wearing a girdle, why you aren't sucking in the way she taught you thirty years ago, and how dare you come into the house of the Lord that way. Your mother, who complains of women in the church nowadays committing the sin of visible panty lines, reminds you that she raised you better than this.

And you say, "I'm tired of holding my breath." Then you promise you won't come to church that way again. And you keep your word because you won't go to church again at all.

How do you make love to a physicist? You send him an apology in the form of one of the many sketches of him you have made, in a silver frame. He doesn't respond right away. And you're okay with that; you knew the risk you ran, disappearing the way you did. But when he does reach out, you're both quiet on the phone for a long time before you say, "It's just something I had to do. For me. I didn't have the words for it then, and I'm not entirely sure I do now."

"I need you to use your words, though," he says. "If we're going to do this, I need you to try. And I promise I won't ever do anything to make you regret trying."

You try to remember the last time a man made you a promise. You decide it doesn't even matter. This man is making you one now. That's what matters.

How do you make love to a physicist? On March 13, the night before he comes to town, you stay up late, taking turns playing old-school hip hop and R&B music videos, talking smack about who's going to get served at your dance-off, Googling your astrological compatibility—your Virgo to his Aquarius—laughing, giddy.

Then Pi Day arrives and you shower while he's en route to the airport. Once he's in the air, his six-hour flight (including layover) feels to you like an eternity. His walk from the plane to your car at curbside takes as long as a pilgrimage. You imagine him kissing the western wall of Sbarro, weeping at the Cinnabon, leaving an offering at the feet of Auntie Anne.

After he drops his luggage into your trunk and closes it, he turns to you and says, "Finally." And you say, "Finally." And he draws you into his arms and kisses you. His lips are as soft as you thought they would be.

At your place, you make omelets and home fries, which he devours. His appetite is magnificent. Then, even though you're both exhausted and sleep deprived, adrenaline kicks in and you win the dance-off by a mile. This man cannot dance to save his life, despite talking much shit.

"What's my prize?" you ask.

Eric pulls you down to the couch and kisses you again. "Oh, so we both win," you say. "Here's a participation trophy." You go in for more kisses, and you think, *God, let him be forever.*

You both begin to doze. At some point you wake up, with your head in his lap and your mind in overdrive. You think about your art show opening tomorrow. You imagine looking at him from across the gallery floor as he looks at your work; introducing him to your girlfriends, your colleagues, your students. And your mother. You think that even if today and tomorrow were all there was, that would be okay. But then you hear your therapist's voice asking what you *feel*, not think, right now. And you struggle at first to find the words before settling on *warm, hopeful, joyous, full.*

Eric strokes your furrowed brows until your face relaxes. You say, "Rumi said, 'Lovers don't finally meet somewhere. They're in each other all along.' Do you believe that?"

"I don't know," he says, then yawns. "Sounds like a mystic's take on fated love, and I don't believe in fate."

You deflate a little. You want him to be the one you've been waiting for, and you want him to feel the inevitability of you as well. You want to be his default, not an option. You want the promises of a new religion.

You chide yourself for walking too far ahead—for regressing into eighties song lyrics territory so soon.

But then he says, "The supermassive black hole at the center of the Milky Way recently sparked seventy-five times brighter over the course of a two-hour period, and twice as bright as it's ever been in the twenty years astronomers have been monitoring it."

By now, you're used to him talking science, but you're not sure where he's going with this.

"One theory," he continues, "is that the event was caused by a star about fifteen times bigger than the Sun getting close to the edge of the black hole, disturbing some gases, heating things up, increasing the infrared radiation coming from the edge. But get this: we observed that star getting close to the black hole about a year before we observed the effects on the black hole."

"That shows just how vast the universe is, how enormous the distance," you say.

"Exactly. Distances, plural. The distance between the star and the edge of the black hole, and the distance between the black hole and Earth. So . . . I say all of this to say that sometimes wheels are set in motion long before the spark is manifest. Is that the same thing as fate? I don't know, but I do know that rare, brilliant events take time."

He sighs. "Which is why I didn't trip when you didn't respond to my messages at first. I figured if you'd wanted me to leave you alone you would've said so. But you didn't. Now I did trip a little when you ghosted me, but"—he shrugs and pulls you closer—"I figured you had your reasons."

How do you make love to a physicist? When he unbuttons your blouse and asks, "Are we going to be the type of people who sit around talking about Rumi and black holes, or are we going to get naked?" you answer, "Both."

You stand up and pull down your skirt and panties. "Rumi wrote of an intuitive love of God, and he was a Muslim," you say. "But people like to strip away the Islam from his work."

He runs his hands over your thighs, your breasts, your free stomach.

How do you make love to a physicist? With your whole self, quivering, lush, unafraid.

JAEL

I THINK the pastor's wife was a freak before she got into the church. She real dark-skin with long, thick hair that she wear in a bun under a black church hat, the wide kind with the feathers. Sometimes the hat is dark blue, or white on Easter. But I bet when she was 14 like me, she used to have a big Afro and wear tight bell-bottoms, like Thelma on Good Times. It's something about the way her eyes sparkle and dance, instead of trying to look all holy. Like she's remembering something fun from a long time ago. And that half-smile of hers. Like her secrets got secrets. And she got them big dick-sucking lips. Twan said that I got them too. But fuck him. Anyway. Everyone calls the preacher's wife "Sister Sadie." In my head, I call her "Sweet Sadie," like that song Kachelle's mama used to play all the time when we were little. But there ain't nothing sweet about that lady. She dress all proper in a buttoned-up suit when she standing up there with the old as dirt Reverend collecting that love offering. Sweet Sadie ain't old-old. Her husband probably 105. She probably 40. Her body reminds me of the album covers Kachelle uncle have in his room. Ohio Players, Lakeside, The Gap Band, Parliament-Funkadelic. They got all these ladies, some real, some cartoons, with big titties, big booties, and dick-sucking lips. Sweet Sadie try to hide all that under them churchy suits. But I bet she used to wear coochie-cutter shorts before she met Old Reverend. She might be fooling the church people, but she ain't fooling me. I know her body is beautiful underneath them suits. I wish I could see it.

—

My mama used to say, "Careful you go looking for something. You just might find it." But I wasn't looking for anything when I went into my great-grandbaby's room not too long ago to change her bed linens and flip her mattress. I really wasn't. I just wanted to air her room out and whatnot, and I always flip the mattresses twice a year, at the same time we turn the clocks forward or back and change the batteries in the smoke detector like they tell you to do. So I flipped the mattress and found her diary. It wasn't too much in the beginning. Just who she didn't like at school, and who didn't like her. Which teachers was mean, and which ones she could charm. I didn't approve of some of her language. But that ain't nothing compared to things I saw about midway through it. Unnatural things. Things that just break my heart. God ain't in this child, even though I trained her up in the way that she should go in hopes that she would not depart from it when she is old. But from the looks of things in that diary, she done departed a long time ago.

—

KACHELLE TOLD him we're 16. That's a bigger lie for me than it is for her. She just turned 15 last week. I still have to wait 6 more months. But he probably don't care how old we really are. He claim he want us to come over to his house for a crab boil in his backyard. Just the 3 of us. Kachelle said she kind of scared. Cause he 35. But she gonna go because he cute. She say he look like Morris Day from The Time who she been in love with ever since "Purple Rain." She dragged me to that movie four times since it came out. I like Prince, but Kachelle is IN LOVE with him and Morris Day too. She say she horny for light-skin niggas. Don't matter either way to me. Niggas is niggas. Light-skin, dark-skin. Fifteen, twenty-five, thirty-five. All the same and none of 'em worth a damn. But Kachelle the type that have to learn the hard way. She all excited about this nigga and a crab boil. And he say he gon take us to the beach, and she all excited about that too, knowing good and well I don't like the beach. I just want to see the inside of that big house of his. See what he got in there.

I wish I could go to Sweet Sadie's house . . . without Old Rev there, of course.

—

I DON'T know how to talk to this child. These kids today . . . they is different than how we was, coming up. What do I say to her that won't get her face all crumpled up out of shape? Littlest thing I say set her off. I tell her to pick up behind herself, put her dishes in the sink at least, make up her bed, put her dirty clothes in the hamper. And she get mad. Just get all bent out of shape if I say anything to her. Sucking her teeth, or acting like she don't even hear me half the time.

The only way I know how to fight the battle for this child's salvation is to give it to the Lord. I pray for her. I do.

Every time she write in that diary, it gets worser and worser. I wish I had the right words to say. I pray to God to touch my mouth so that I can speak, and to touch her ears, heart, and mind so that she can hear.

Because God knows I don't want no abomination living under my roof.

No, these kids today not like we was. We respected our elders. We ain't sass and talk back. We did what we were told to do, and you only had to tell us once. None of this, "In a minute . . ." We didn't have to be told twice. And if we did, we got the back of my mama's hand for our troubles.

But I don't hit this child no more. I can count on one hand the number of times I whupped her in her fourteen years on this earth and in my home, and I made sure that nobody else hit her either. There was enough hitting going on between her mama and her trifling daddy when she was just a lil bitty thing, which is how she come to live with me. So I didn't want to do it if I didn't have to, but she just has this way about her . . . Like she don't respond to words she don't like. She didn't even respond the way I wanted her to when I braided them switches and tore up them skinny, yella legs of hers when she was little. It's like she didn't even feel it. Didn't cry a lick. One time, when she was six and I took the switch to them legs, she just looked at me . . . just give me this look that froze my blood and sent me straight to my Bible. "Behold, I give unto you power to tread on serpents and scorpions, and over all the power of the enemy: and nothing shall by any means hurt you." Luke 10:19.

And I stay in my Bible, I stay on my knees and prayed up over this child. I thank the Lord that she not fast in the behind like that lil friend of hers, chasing after grown men. But she still ain't right, sitting up there with me in service every Sunday after Sunday School and then Bible study on Wednesday night. Every week. Sit right there and don't say a word. And to look at her, you wouldn't know. She look sweet in the face. Folks think she just quiet. But in her heart, her spirit, her mind . . . That ain't of God. There is a battle going on, saints. I stay in my Bible and on my knees as a prayer warrior for this child's soul. "For we wrestle not against flesh and blood, but against principalities, against powers, against the rulers of the darkness of this world, against spiritual wickedness in high places." Ephesians 6:12.

—

SWEET SADIE talked to me at church today! She asked me how I was doing and how Granny's doing. I told her we're doing fine, and I didn't even mind that she kind of had that look on her face that people get when they talking to The Girl With The Dead Parents. Pity. I hate that shit. But it wasn't so bad with Sweet Sadie. I feel like she really care.

—

ONE THING I can say good about her: she ain't letting none of them boys mess with her, far as I can tell. They don't come sniffing around here like they did with her mama and her mama's mama, my daughter, God rest their souls. And I was up at the corner store the other day getting some Goody powders, and I overheard two fellas in the checkout line talking about her. Either they didn't see me, or didn't know I'm her grandmama. And the one fella say to the other one, "My man told me some girl kicked that nigga Jay's ass."

And the other one say, "Naw, man. It was Jay's lil brother, Twan. And it didn't happen like that, but it was some wild shit. That Jael, man. That lil redbone that live over on Perkins? That bitch crazy. Twan said ever since they were in grade school, she'd fight dudes for trying to grab her ass. She been going toe-to-toe with dudes around the block for years. So he figure, she must like girls, right?"

"Like what? A bulldagger," the other one say.

"Yeah, man!" And then he lowered his voice, but I could still hear him. "You know I hollered at her a couple of times around here. Cause she fine."

Now these fellas had to be thirty, thirty-five years old. Just filthy.

"So me and Jay and Twan were standing outside the store that day," he say, "and here she come down the sidewalk with her friend. Twan figure she not gon' try to kick his ass with us standing there too, right?"

"Right, right . . ."

"Twan called her name, and she ignored him. Just kept walking past. So he called her a bulldagger and ran up behind her and grabbed her ass. Maaan, she swung around with a bottle, smashed it against the wall, and had it at that nigga's throat!"

"Redbones is crazy, man." That's what the other one said.

Then the first fella say, "I didn't even see that bottle! It just came outta nowhere! She ain't stab him, but that's just cuz her friend—the one with the big titties? Lachelle? Kachelle!—she just started screaming, 'He ain't worth it! He ain't worth it!' But man, she was gonna do it. Jael crazy."

That's right, baby. Let 'em think you crazy. Let them think you don't like boys, even though that is unnatural in the eyes of God. Least they leave you alone that way.

But maybe she really is crazy.

They say bad seeds skip a generation. My daughter Timna was just like Jael. Just looked right through you. Her best friend, a sweet, pretty girl named Gloria Mae, got killed by a train, and Timna never shed a tear. Not a single one. The two of them was playing around on the tracks—after I told them a million times to stay off them tracks—and poor Gloria Mae didn't get out of the way in time. Sixteen years old . . . Lord, rest her soul. And you'd think a person would be sad to lose a friend, to see 'em die like that. But not Timna. She just wasn't fazed. Just floated through life for years all closed up in herself until the Lord just took her one day. Walking home in the rain from her job down at Woolworth's, struck by lightning, twenty-four years old. I told her a million times not to walk out in them thunderstorms, to get a gypsy cab and I'd pay the carfare, but she was hardheaded. And a decade after she died, here comes Jael, just like her.

And Jael's mother, Keturah, that child wasn't built for this world. I raised her from the time she was six, when Timna died. I did the best I could. But in the end, she let that nigga, Jael's daddy, beat on her until he killed her. Wasn't even her husband, just some no 'count Negro.

But here comes this fat yella baby, head full of good, curly hair. Eyes bright as buttons. But just like my Timna, she looked right through you. And just like my Timna, I give her everything I have. I have spared her the ugliness about her daddy and what happened to her mama. I am the only mother she has ever known. And she has wanted for nothing.

I tried, with Keturah and Jael, to do the things my mother did for us. Tried to teach them things, like how to cook a pot of rice just right, how to frost a cake without tearing it up, how to wash and fold laundry, how to make the bed, how to keep theyself clean. Keturah took to it all, loved baking and frying chicken and helping me out in the kitchen. She laughed easy and never talked back. She was a good girl. But then that nigga came along and took her away from here.

Jael is different. She'll cook and clean and do whatever I ask, for the most part. But there is no joy in those bright eyes, not even when she was little. It's like her body is in one place, but her spirit is somewhere else altogether. It's always been that way. Now sometimes she will come in my room and watch my stories with me. She likes *The Young and the Restless*. And some Friday nights, she'll watch my TV programs with me. *Dallas* and *Falcon Crest*. But most nights? I have to make her sit down and eat dinner with me. She live in her own world and keep me shut out of it.

Well, at least she don't give none of these boys the time-a day. Unlike her lil fast-tail friend Kachelle. Jael not impressed by this high-yella nigga what she call "Morris Day," come sniffing 'round these young girls. I know his type. Lord Jesus, I know that type too well. One thing always lead to another with them. Make you feel like the Queen of Sheba, like you the only one. You say stop, they act like you said go.

My old neighbor Miss Maybelle used to yell at us from her front porch, "Don't let the boys fool ya." We just thought she was a crazy old lady tryna keep us from having our fun, you know.

But she knew. She knew. And we didn't listen. I think sometimes how things mighta been if I had listened. Probably wouldn't be no Timna, no Keturah, no Jael. Just me in the world. Doing what, I don't know. Something.

Anyway. Jael ain't said a word to me 'bout Twan or that crab boil that this Morris Day is supposed to be having. But she don't tell me nothing. Just do what she want to do.

—

CAN YOU suck dicks and still be saved? I'm just wondering. I don't care about dicks or being saved. Tracy round the corner suck dick all the time. But she'll do anything, so you can't go by her. Kachelle uncle had this white girlfriend, and Kachelle used to see her doing it on their back porch when they thought everybody was sleep. Kachelle says that sucking dick is nasty, and she will never do it. Kachelle is always talking about what she's never going to do. I asked her if she like girls. Maybe she want to do things with girls. She got mad and said that that wasn't funny. I said I wasn't trying to be funny. And if she like girls that wouldn't bother me. But she wouldn't listen. Just shook her head and started crying about how she's a good girl. Kachelle is a big crybaby. If I wasn't around, people would mess with her even more than they already do. Anyway.

Today at church, Old Rev was talking about how you have to be saved and give up the sinful pleasures of the flesh if you want to get to heaven. Seem like saved folks don't like to do anything but talk about being saved, complain about sin, and go to church. And church be boring as hell, so I just watch Sweet Sadie and think about her sexy body and her secret past.

—

I NEED the Lord to give me a sign. I want to stay in His will. But what is worse? Jael not coming to church, or coming with a reprobate mind? That's what our Bible study was about this week: "And even as they did not like to retain God in their knowledge, God gave them over to a reprobate mind, to do those things which are not convenient; being filled with all unrighteousness, fornication, wickedness, covetousness, maliciousness; full of envy, murder, debate, deceit, malignity; whisperers, backbiters, haters of God, despiteful, proud, boasters, inventors of evil things, disobedient to parents, without understanding, covenant-breakers, without natural affection, implacable, unmerciful: who knowing the judgment of God, that they which commit such things are worthy of death, not only do the same, but have pleasure in them that do them." Romans 1:28–32.

That is Jael to a T. Full of debate, deceit, and

malignity. And disobedient! At a certain point, if you just willful about your sin, God will give you over to a reprobate mind. As Deacon Sharpe explained this Scripture on Wednesday night, I looked at Jael out the corner of my eye. She had that blank look on her face at first, but then she smiled a little. And for a second, I thought Jesus had heard my cry and worked a miracle in her heart. But then I followed her eyes. She was smiling at Sister Sadie! And it was just like the Scripture say: *wickedness, without natural affection*. I could see it! But I don't think anyone else could see it. Probably just looked like an innocent smile to them, because they don't know the things I know, the unspeakable things she wrote about Sister Sadie in that diary.

Sister Sadie happened to look up at that moment and smiled back at Jael. Not that I blame Sister Sadie for just being polite and kind to an orphaned child. Jesus said to feed the orphans and the widows. But I know my Savior would not approve of the thoughts of this particular orphan.

Well. I made up my mind right then and there. I am not going to wake her up for church come Sunday morning, and no more Wednesday night Bible study either. She will not do her wickedness in Greater Holiness Baptist Church. Not as long as I draw breath in my body.

I just hope the Lord understands why I'm keeping her out of His house.

—

I DON'T like Morris Day. Turns out his real name is Jamie, a girl name. But I don't know which name is worse because "Morris Day" makes me think of Morris the picky cat in the commercial. And come to think of it, he kinda looks like a yellow tabby cat. Gray cat eyes, whiskers. I've seen thicker mustaches on boys in my grade. He's not even as cute as the real Morris Day. And he smokes cigarettes, so his breath smells horrible. And his house ain't nothing special either. It's got two floors, but the rooms are tiny. He's got one room he calls a Florida room. It just look like a living room to me. And the rooms are crammed full of shit that belonged to his dead mother. She had terrible taste and she liked to make ceramic cats. I counted 50 fucking cats before I gave up. The crabs were good though. Real hot and salty, big chunks of meat, like I like them. Granny makes shitty crabs. Watery with no taste. Not worth all the hassle it takes to get at the stringy meat. She buys the teeny-weeny ones.

Morris Day/Jamie bought the big crabs that cost $8 a dozen. When he was dropping them in the pot, Kachelle was hiding behind me like she was scared. He grabbed one of the crabs with some tongs and played like he was going to put it on her. She started screaming and ran upstairs. Morris/Jamie ran up after her still holding the crab. After a minute, I thought Kachelle was going to run back down, but she didn't. So I went upstairs. The crab was at the top of the stairs crawling toward me. I kicked it down the stairs back to the first floor. I heard a crack when it landed. When I turned around, Kachelle was coming out of one of the bedrooms, grinning like an idiot. Morris/Jamie was right behind her, still holding the stupid tongs, sweating like a crackhead. And the whole time we ate the crabs in the backyard, he was sweating. So greasy and disgusting. And he kept cracking jokes that wasn't even funny. But Kachelle laughed all loud like he was Eddie Murphy.

When we walked home after, I waited for her to tell me something, but she didn't. So I said, He sweat like a pig, and he ain't even cute. And his house is full of junk. Kachelle just rolled her eyes and told me I don't like nobody and she'll talk to me later. That was four days ago. I called her a couple of times and Miss Debra said she wasn't home. And she still hasn't called me back.

I took the long way back from the store yesterday, cut through the field behind the high school, and walked past Jamie's house. He was in the driveway washing his Cadillac, which is really his dead mother's Cadillac. A cigarette dangled between his lips like it was gonna fall any second. And he was sweating like a pig, as usual, even though he was wearing an undershirt with no sleeves. His arms were soft and pale. No muscles in sight. Soft-ass nigga. I pretended like I didn't see him, but he hollered Hey, Pretty Girl at me. I ignored him and kept walking. Then he said, You just missed your friend. She just left. He kept on talking and I kept on walking.

Fuck Kachelle and her bad taste in men.

—

NEVER IN all my days have I known a child so ungrateful. She has never known a hungry day in her life, not in my house. I bet she wouldn't be so high and mighty in somebody's foster care, which is where her behind would've ended up if I hadn't taken her in out of the goodness of my heart. I raised my child and outlived her. My grandchild too. I believe I have earned some rest on this earth and my crown in heaven. But where else was she going to go? I do my best to make ends meet, and this lil heffa says I make shitty crabs?

Well. When she brings her tail back here from wherever she run off to this afternoon, I got something for her. It's time for her to get a job.

—

ME AND Kachelle went to the beach with Jamie. Kachelle called him her goddaddy and she had on a new yellow bathing suit he bought her. He lifted her up high in the air and she screamed and laughed as he threw her into the waves over and over again. Kachelle is not a small girl. So I guess he's stronger than those weak-ass arms of his look. Then they got tired of that game, and Kachelle climbed up and rode on Jamie's shoulders as he walked farther out into the ocean. I couldn't see, but I imagined his hands clutching Kachelle's thighs. Every now and then, her body would shake. From laughing probably. They got so far away, I couldn't hear her anymore.

It was hot, but not too bad under the umbrella Jamie rented. I sat on a blanket with a People magazine I picked up when we had stopped at 7–11 to get soda, ice, sunflower seeds, and potato chips. I had already told Kachelle I wasn't getting in the water because I didn't have a bathing suit. She said, You can get in with your shorts on. They'll dry. I just rolled my eyes. She's so dumb. But Jamie stood next to her nodding like she was just the smartest girl in the whole wide world.

When we walked down the boardwalk heading to the beach, we passed a shop selling beach stuff. Kachelle grabbed a pair of white sunglasses, some yellow flip-flops, and a huge towel with different color fish on it. She handed everything to Jamie and he paid for it. They had bathing suits too, right next to the cash register. Jamie didn't offer to buy me one. Not that I would've taken it.

The water came up to Jamie's neck at one point because I could only see Kachelle. It looked like she was sitting on top of the waves. Then she tumbled backward off Jamie's shoulders and waves covered them both. When I could see their heads again, they were facing each other and Kachelle had her arms wrapped around Jamie's shoulders. How could she stand his nasty cigarette breath that close up? UGH. I couldn't see for the water, but I bet her legs were probably wrapped around his back. Then they both looked back at me. I lifted the People magazine to cover my face.

To hell with them.

I started daydreaming about Sweet Sadie. I bet she had come to the beach lots of times before she became a preacher's wife. I imagine her riding down the shoreline on the back of some big dude's motorcycle. Wearing a white bikini, which looks so good against her brown, brown skin. And the dude, I picture him wearing dark shades and a denim jacket with no sleeves that shows off his muscles. But when they start to pass me, Sadie tells him to stop and let her off the motorcycle. She stomps through the sand toward me and reaches out her hands. I try not to stare at her titties falling out of the top of the bikini, but she notices and just laughs. She pulls me up off the blanket and hugs me. She smells like vanilla and roses. And she keeps hugging me and we start walking, walking, walking down the shore.

And then I feel the water on my feet and pull away.

I run back to the blanket I brought from home. Sweet Sadie sits next to me and says, What's wrong? And I tell her about the water. About how I run showers and baths that I never get into to make Granny think I'm bathing. I just do what Granny call a birdbath, at the sink. I get clean from head to toe like that. Just takes a lot of scrubbing and rinsing. And I tell her about the day my mama died and how I saw it all underwater. We were all under the water. My mama, my daddy, and me. We were in our house, in the bedroom, and I was in my crib. Underwater. Sweet Sadie says, How can you remember so much as a baby? I say, I don't know how. I just do. And I saw what he did. And I tried to scream but the water filled my mouth and then everything went black. Granny lied to me. She said they were killed in a car accident. But one time when I was 8, I heard Auntie Vashti tell Granny that somebody slit his throat in prison and let him bleed out like the animal he was. Auntie sighed real sad and said he had seemed like such a nice boy. Granny said she knew from jump he wasn't no good, but my mama didn't know it because he had her nose wide open . . .

I remember his face that day in our house. Tight and mean. We were underwater that day, but I remember it.

Sweet Sadie rubs my arm and calls me Baby Girl. Baby Girl, she says, you weren't underwater. Those were your tears.

I looked up over the top of the magazine, and the daydream was over. Jamie was walking back to shore with Kachelle on his back. When they got back to me and the umbrella, Kachelle's head still rested on his shoulder, like she never wanted to let go.

On the ride home, Kachelle sat in the back seat with me. I was still mad that she had sat in the front seat on the ride to the beach. Jamie lit up another damn cigarette and I rolled the window down and let the wind hit my face. Then I heard Kachelle call my name real soft. WHAT? I asked her, real loud. She kept whispering. Telling me to remember what she told me when she woke me up, calling from Jamie's house early in the morning. That if her mama asked, we took the bus to the beach at 8:00 in the morning.

The truth was, she didn't call me back to ask me to come to the beach with them until 1:00.

I turned my back on her and pretended I was sleep.

—

It's time to toss out that old throw rug in my living room. I been meaning to get rid of it. I got myself so worked up fussing with Jael about getting a job that I must've tripped over that rug. Yeah, that had to be it. I must've lost my balance. I was fussing, then I just felt myself falling, and the next thing you know, I was on my hands and knees. I must've tripped on that old rug. Or maybe it was that *vertigo*, I think they call it. My friend Alma gets it from time to time. That had to be it.

I was there on the floor, and Jael just looked down at me. Didn't offer to help me up or nothing! And I can't even repeat what she said to me when I told her to start looking for a job.

I crawled over to the settee and pulled myself up. And that girl just stood there and watched me struggle.

And ever since then, she stay holed up in her room. She came out to get a plate of food a few times and to wash up, but that's it.

Yes, I lied to her about her mama and her daddy. But Lord knows I was just trying to protect her from the ugliness. He knows my heart.

Maybe I could try and talk to her about that, now that she's older. But she won't come out of the room. She wouldn't even come to the phone when that Kachelle called. Just kept calling and calling, till the girl finally came to the house. Jael wouldn't even talk to her through the bedroom door. Kachelle came in here talking all sweet to me like butter wouldn't melt in her mouth. *Granny D this, Granny D that*. I started to tell her, "If I was ya granny, you wouldn't be the hussy you are." But I asked Jesus to bind my tongue and He answered.

—

KACHELLE SWORE on Miss Debra's Bible that all that time she was alone at Jamie's house before we went to the beach, all she let him do was kiss her. I said, Yeah, kiss you WHERE? And she got all mad. I didn't want to talk to her for a long time after that day at the beach. I couldn't shake the feeling that she was lying to me. And I'm sick and tired of people lying to me. But I guess me and Kachelle are friends again. I worry about her more than I'm mad at her. But when she does stuff to make me worry, that makes me mad! Being friends with someone who can't look out for themselves is a lot of work and I'm tired. But Kachelle would just say, I can look out for myself! But she can't. I know she can't. She ain't built for it.

So I finally said yes when she asked me for the fifty-leventh time to spend the night at her house. She called Jamie a couple of times while I was there. They talked about him taking her shopping for school clothes next week. I asked her how she was going to explain new clothes to Miss Debra and she covered the phone receiver and shushed me. Then I asked her does she make Jamie brush his filthy cigarette mouth before they kiss, and she dragged the phone into the closet and shut the door. I guess I was just supposed to entertain myself while they gabbed away.

We laid in Kachelle's bed later, talking, but I didn't say half the things I was thinking. She kept going on about Jamie this and Jamie that. And how boys her age just want to fuck her, and have the nerve to not even be cute. How Jamie was happy just to kiss her and spend time with her and spend money on her. And how he didn't make her do anything she didn't want to do. I wondered how long that was going to last, not making her do things. How long before he turned into someone else and hurt her? But I kept all that to myself.

Then she said, Why you being so quiet? You jealous? And I said, OF WHO? No answer. Then I asked her a question. I said, Do you think heaven is a real place? She said, Of course it is. Then I said, I think heaven is a lie. And she sat up in the bed and said, God is going to strike you down for talking like that, Jael! I just laughed and told her God is just a white man stupid niggas made up, like Santa Claus. Well, she didn't like that one bit. She folded her arms across her chest and said, Well if there ain't no God, then answer me this. Where do people go when they . . .

She couldn't even say the word "die," with her scary ass. I just laughed and turned over in the bed. And then we were just quiet until we fell asleep.

The next evening, I was walking back home and went past Jamie's house again. He was in his front yard watering the grass with the hose. The sun had went down so it was kinda cool and he wasn't sweating for once. He said, Hey, Pretty Girl. And I said hey back. He said, You always going somewhere in a hurry. Stop by and see me sometime.

I said, Okay.

—

THIS IS all my fault. I picked the child's name from the Bible, at random, but I was the one that picked it. My mother and her mother before her and her mother before her, my sisters and my aunts and their children . . . we all had our names chose out the Bible. The oldest woman in the family would open the big family Bible and point her finger on the page. Whatever woman's name was closest to her finger that was the name of the girl-child to be born. And we kept turning pages and pointing until we found a woman's name. All we ever birth were girls. For seven generations, nothing but girls. If I believed in luck, and if our lives had turned out better than how they did, I'd say it was a lucky seven. Even still, I sometimes play a bunch of sevens in the lotto. Just every once in a while, no regular thing. Because maybe the sevens is a message from the Lord. Folks like to say, "God moves in mysterious ways, His wonders to perform." But that ain't Scripture. That's a hymn. It's Romans 11:33 that says, "O the depth of the riches both of the wisdom and knowledge of God! How unsearchable are his judgments, and his ways past finding out!"

Playing them sevens helped keep my lights on a time or two. Lord can't be mad at that. Seven generations of us. Dorcas in 1871. Adah in 1890. Adah's five daughters: Chloe, Mara, Shelomith, Salome, and in 1906, my mother, Matred. Damaris, me, 1922, and my younger sisters, Vashti, Euodia, and Cozbi. My daughter, Timna, in 1937. Jael's mother, Keturah, in 1955. And a bunch of nieces, great-nieces, and cousins, I forget. I used-ta could name us all.

I named her Jael. My finger landed right on top of the name. Usually I had to look around the page until I found a name for a girl, or start over on another page. But that time, I landed right on it. I was so excited by that, thinking it was a sign that this child would be blessed. That she would be different. I didn't stop to read the story of Jael in the Bible, not till much later.

Maybe if I had read it, I mighta chose a different name. But probably not. What I look like going against six generations of tradition? We never talked about the stories behind the names. The name picked was the name given.

When Jael was first taking the bus to school, some of the kids would tease her, call her "Jailbird," especially that Twan. He one of Verdine

Russell's ill-mannered grandsons. He'd follow her home from the bus stop, and I'd hear him out front there, calling her "Jailbird! Jailbird!" And the other kids would laugh and join in. And that Kachelle told them time and time again, "It's JAH-ell." They kept on. But Jael didn't pay 'em no mind. At the time, I thought she was just doing a good job of ignoring them and leaving them to the Lord like I told her to. But now I know that their teasing just watered that bad seed planted in her.

We would come together for the naming. My mother and her mother, when they were living; my sisters and me; our children and then their children and so on. We'd cook and eat. We'd ask Father God to bless the mother and the girl-child yet to be born. We'd laugh and tell stories. And someone, usually whatever man was around at the time, would always ask, "But what if it's a boy?" And we'd just laugh some more.

Even if we was arguing, fussing, and fighting with each other just the day before, the tradition brought us together. We honored tradition. What else were we going to cling to? We had five living generations when Jael was born because we had our babies young, at fifteen, sixteen, seventeen, eighteen, nineteen. Ain't no shame or pride. Just the way it was. A family full of women, and we had the worst time with men. The good men died young, and the terrible ones stayed just long enough to make you wish they would die. God forgive me.

Some years back, the news people came and did a story on our family reunion. It was on a national program. But now my mama, my aunts, my sisters, my daughter, Jael's mother . . . all gone, 'cept my baby sister Vashti, some cousins, and the nieces and great-nieces. I guess the rest of them just naming their babies any old thing now because I don't hear from 'em. Maybe even had some sons. Who knows?

Jael was the last one I named. And she is my cross to bear.

And I named the ones I didn't give birth to, the ones I drank the tea and got rid of, Lord Jesus, forgive me. Anah. Shimeath. Ruth. Baara.

—

CIGARETTE MOUTH didn't taste as bad as I thought it would. Or maybe because I had something else on my mind, I didn't care. In the end, it would be worth it. The cigarettes Jamie kept smoking made me want to gag, though. But I didn't. I just smiled at him through the smoke.

We had been on the couch kissing for a while. Then Jamie said it was starting to get dark and maybe I should leave before Granny got worried. Plus he had to get up at 3 in the morning for work.

He worked at the Sunbeam bread factory. I told him that Granny wouldn't be home from Bible study for at least another hour. And that we could do more than just kiss. He asked me if I had done more, with somebody else. I said no, which is the truth. Jamie asked me if I was going to tell Kachelle. I said I don't tell her my business. He gave a tiny little smile like he really liked that answer but didn't want to let on. And I told him that. He laughed and said, You don't miss anything, do you?

He started to push me back on the couch. I asked him if he had a rubber. He looked all disappointed and said, Yeah. He got up to go and I told him to brush his teeth while he was at it. He laughed and said, Girl, you a trip.

By the time he finished brushing and came back with the rubber, I was standing in his front yard. It was dark out there and quiet. Jamie came outside and asked me, What's the matter? He didn't say it in a mad way. Kinda in a whisper. I told him nothing was the matter. I just changed my mind and I better get home. He nodded real slow and said okay and that I was welcome anytime.

When I walked home, it was like all the thoughts in my head were competing to be first. I couldn't hold on to one at a time. When I turned the corner onto my street, one thought finally won out: Sweet Sadie. I hadn't seen her in a while ever since Granny started leaving for church without me. But I think about her a lot and I miss her.

—

I SLEPT through it. I hadn't been sleeping too well these last couple of weeks, but I took a pill as soon as I got home from Bible study, and it knocked me right out. But Barbara next door said she heard it, woke her out of a dead sleep, just a little after three this morning. She said it was a big *boom*! And she thought it was thunder and then rolled over and went back to sleep. But then she heard the sirens.

Some kind of gas leak is what the police said, from a gas stove. It was on the news this morning. They said his name was Jamie McWhite, but they didn't have no picture. My mother was friends with some McWhites long ago when I was a girl. Barbara said he was that light-skin one drive the white Cadillac around here. Said his mother—rest her soul—her last name was Porter and that was her house he was living in. Now I remember her from way back when, but I didn't know her to have no kids. Barbara said Jamie's daddy raised him, over on the east side. That's why I didn't know him. But Barbara know a woman what live down the street from him, and she told Barbara that every time she saw him, he had a cigarette in his mouth. And cigarettes and gas don't mix.

Good thing he lived at a dead end and the property next to his was vacant. Barbara say there was a little damage to the houses behind his, but "no other fatalities" is what the news said.

Jael did something this morning she ain't done in years. She climbed in my bed with me and went back to sleep.

A little while later that Kachelle started calling on the phone for Jael, sounding sad. Just calling and calling all day. But Jael shook her head no when I tried to hand her the phone. Finally, about the tenth time that lil hussy called, I just told her, "God don't like ugly," and hung up the phone. She ain't call no more after that.

But I want to talk to Jael too. I still don't know what to say to her. This child thought she was doing the right thing. And yes, he was a nasty, nasty man. But the Bible clearly say, "Thou shalt not kill" and "Vengeance is mine, sayeth the Lord." And what if the woman Barbara knows saw Jael leaving that house yesterday? What if she tells the police?

Maybe Jael can tell the police how he was messing around with her and that Kachelle. People would understand what kind of person he was.

But what if they don't? What if they say Jael is a fast-tail girl who . . . ?

Lord Jesus, give me the right words to say to this child and give her ears to hear!

And watch over me, Father God.

—

I'M GOING to set my alarm clock to get up Sunday morning and go to church with Granny. Wanna see Sister Sadie again. For real and not just in my dreams.

Granny always say, Every shut eye ain't sleep. And that's how I am. I don't tell everything I know. I keep some stuff to myself. Sometimes forever, sometimes till the time is right. I just let people think I don't know what's going on. And then, when they least expect it . . . I strike.

But it doesn't have to be that way. As long as people keep their mouths shut, leave me alone, and mind their business, it doesn't have to be that way at all.

—

Extolled above women be Jael,
The wife of Heber the Kenite,
Extolled above women in the tent.
He asked for water, she gave him milk;
She brought him cream in a lordly dish.
She stretched forth her hand to the nail,
Her right hand to the workman's hammer,
And she smote Sisera; she crushed his head,
She crashed through and transfixed his
temples.

At her feet he curled himself, he fell, he lay
still;
At her feet he curled himself, he fell;
And where he curled himself, let it be,
there he fell dead.

—*Song of Deborah*, Judges 5:24–27

INSTRUCTIONS FOR MARRIED CHRISTIAN HUSBANDS

—

THE BASICS

You, the infantilized husbands of accomplished godly women, are especially low-hanging fruit. Ripe for the picking with little effort on my part. Buttery soft laughter at your attempts at humor, or eye contact that lasts a beat too long but subtle enough that it leaves you wondering if maybe you just imagined it was a beat too long. Maybe it was just wishful thinking on your part that I leaned in closer each time you spoke, that I was really tuned in to and turned on by your monologues on fantasy football and barbecue. Or maybe you just want a woman to treat you like a man for a change, and not like one of her children.

Despite your frustrations, you may not want to stray. Perhaps this is your first time. And you didn't imagine it would be with someone like me—dark with short, kinky hair. Someone so different from your wife. But it was my eyes, my lips, my teeth, my smile, my intellect, my breasts, my easy laughter that got you. I understand you feel the need to offer some explanation for stepping out with someone like me, some reason for why I turn you on.

Why do you turn me on? It's that you want me when there are so many reasons you shouldn't. *That* turns me on. Your hunger, your deprivation turn me on. I don't care why your wife won't fuck you properly; it's satisfaction enough simply knowing she won't. All the risk is yours, but I'll wade out into it with you. I've always enjoyed playing in the deep end.

PARKING

There is on-street parking in my neighborhood. I recommend you park at least one block away. The nearby business district provides a convenient alibi.

SOCIAL MEDIA AND TECHNOLOGY

Facebook: Continue to post Scripture memes about God's faithfulness and how Jesus is your all in all, if you do that sort of thing. If you don't, don't start now. See also "Your Religion" below.

Because this town is small, Facebook may recommend me as a Person You May Know. I hope it goes without saying that you should delete this.

Post a picture of your wife on Woman Crush

Wednesdays #wcw, but be sure to caption it that she is your crush every day. Also post pictures of the two of you on your anniversary, her birthday, and at other random times, just to say how amazing she is. Your profile picture should be a picture of the two of you.

Communication: We will not exchange phone numbers. We will communicate exclusively via the texting app I asked you to download.

Your phone: Lock it. Require a passcode or finger-swipe combination to unlock it.

Photos: Don't send them. Don't ask for them.

Note: If you want to get caught, as some of you do because you don't have the courage to pull the plug on your marriage directly, ignore these precautions. See also "Your Conscience."

ABOUT ME

The less you know, the better. And that works both ways. Boundaries are crucial. Here's what I can tell you:

I have no children, and I've never been married. My life is my own. I own a bakery, which is probably where we met. Maybe I baked your wedding cake or your daughter's birthday cake. I make the best peach cobbler in the city.

I grew up watching my mother eating the crumbs

and leftovers from another woman's table. I swore I never would. But here I am grubbing, licking the edges.

HEALTH AND WELLNESS

Bring *original copies only* of your STI test results from tests taken within the last thirty days. No exceptions. No, not even if you haven't been with anyone besides your wife in decades. Surely you understand why I can't take you at your word. No honor among thieves. Or something like that.

If you aren't capable of making an appointment for yourself and getting the testing done, you don't deserve to fuck.

You will wear a condom at all times. This is non-negotiable. If you are unable to get an erection while wearing a condom, go home to your wife.

Note: My baby factory has been closed, surgically, for some time now. No worries there.

YOUR RELIGION

By all means, continue teaching Sunday School, leading the Boy Scout troop, and serving on the deacon board at church.

If guilt gets the best of you, do not attempt to witness to me or invite me to church. Don't ask me to repent, because I regret nothing.

You can't save me, because I'm not in peril.

YOUR WIFE

Don't speak ill of her to me. I don't want to hear about how she just lies there like a starfish during sex or how she emasculates you in front of company. That's a slippery slope to justifying why you're here, and we're not doing that.

You know *her*, but I know women. You assume she would be angry or disappointed to learn you're cheating. But you may be surprised to know some wives are actually relieved. Your wife probably appreciates the peace and quiet of you taking your needs elsewhere. She may actually desire sex, just not with you, not anymore. You may want to explore with a marriage counselor why that is. See also "Therapist."

MONEY

Gifts are welcome, but do not offer me money or to pay my bills. I'm not a sex worker.

SEX

You may spank me and dress me up in trashy lingerie. I find those things tedious and terribly unoriginal, but I will oblige. See also "Fantasies."

I am easily and multiply orgasmic. Understand this has very little to do with your sexual prowess. Physical arousal is easy; I crave mental and intellectual stimulation. Get inside my head. Surprise me. Challenge me.

I'm not overly concerned with your dick, though

it is important. I like hands. I really, really like hands. The bigger, the better. I want to be held, caressed, cupped, and grabbed.

I also like lips and tongues and kissing. Deep, passionate kisses, and biting. I will come if you kiss me right. If you discover my secret place and kiss me there and touch me there just right, I will drown us both.

Note: Do you know what your wife likes and doesn't like? You should.

YOUR CONSCIENCE

If you decide to confess to your wife, make sure she doesn't come over to my house. She will get her feelings hurt. Our arrangement is nonbinding; if you want to leave, go. But don't bring your mess into my yard.

And when you're here, don't dawdle. I hate small talk. Leave your nerves outside my door. Do or don't do; there is no try.

See also "Therapist."

SUBSTANCES

Don't come to me under the influence of anything. You will be fully in control of your faculties and responsible for your actions at all times.

Don't ask me to score drugs either. Not even weed. Ask your cousin, the one everybody in your family says should be more like you.

TRAVEL

I am available to travel with sufficient notice and at your expense.

THERAPIST

I am not yours. I don't want to hear about your fears of failure or inadequacy, childhood traumas, midlife regrets, children, or frustrations with your job. This is one of the safeguards that keeps feelings at bay, and more importantly, it keeps me from resenting you the way your wife does.

YOUR ARRIVAL

Place your wedding band on my nightstand. Your hands may be immaculate, nails tapered. Or they may be rough and dry from the cold, lack of attention, or both. But they must be large, and your grip should always be firm and aggressive.

Remove your cuff links and unbutton your monogrammed shirt. Pull your alma mater or fraternity sweatshirt over your head. Take off the striped polo shirt your kids gave you for Father's Day.

Take off your undershirt. Your chest may be hairy or smooth; your manscaping, or lack thereof, is your business. Your abs may be taut and defined, or you may have dad bod, soft and rounded in places that used to be taut. Or your belly may tell the story of the nightly cognac, gin, or beer you drink to forget. Or to remember.

Slip off your Cole Haan loafers or your Adidas. Take off your socks. Or leave them on.

Toss your jeans, your sweats, your tailored Armani suit pants onto the back of my chair, the foot of my bed, or the floor.

Pull down your boxers or boxer briefs and step out of them. (If you are wearing regular briefs, you will be asked to leave.) Show me that you are ready for me, or that you are not yet ready and would like my assistance.

Silence your phone, or don't.

Regardless of the options you choose above, you will remove the reminder that you don't belong here. Your wedding band must remain on my nightstand, in view at all times. It is your lifesaver. It will keep you from floating away into me for more than a few hours.

FOREPLAY

I understand that sex with your wife is an orchestrated event you prep for, much like surgery. She requires coaxing, compliments, massages, and other romantic gestures to get her in the mood to have sex with you. I require no such thing. I build monuments to my impulses and desires on the backs of men like you.

FANTASIES

We all have a dark side. I invite you to explore

yours with me. I won't judge or shame you, and it goes without saying that all your secrets are safe with me. If you propose something I can't oblige, I'll simply say no, and we'll never speak of it again.

I understand that some fantasies aren't dark. They just . . . are. Same rules apply. No judgment, no shame. Role-playing is a good way to discover what you like. I have some favorites I can share with you, upon request.

FEELINGS

I hate to break it to your ego, but good dick won't cause me to develop feelings for you. If you develop feelings for me, don't worry; the moment will pass.

Under no circumstances should you even think about leaving your marriage for me. You can leave the marriage if you want, but not for me. I'm not waiting in the wings for you to be single. Remember: My reasons for wanting you are predicated on your hunger and the fact that you are off limits. Don't ruin this for me by acting like a lovelorn teenager.

Note: In the event I do start to fall for you, you will know because I'll stop responding to your text messages. This is for the best.

The austere tone of these instructions aside, I actually like you and can't wait to fuck you. If I didn't like you, if the thought of you didn't make my panties wet, we wouldn't be here.

YOUR DEPARTURE

You will leave beyond satisfied. I will treat every time we're together as if it's our last. So many wild cards with men like you, I've learned.

Shower or don't. Gather your things. Leave nothing behind. Slide your ring back onto your finger. Tread until you are back on dry land.

WHEN EDDIE LEVERT COMES

"TODAY IS the day," Mama announced, as she did every day when Daughter came to her room with the breakfast tray.

"Good morning, Mama." Daughter set the tray on the padded bench in front of Mama's vanity. She squinted at the early morning sun shining through the thin curtains. Mama's vanity was covered with powders and bottles of fragrances that hadn't been touched in months.

Mama brushed past Daughter without a word. She opened a chifforobe drawer and took out a navy-and-white-striped short-sleeved blouse. She carried the blouse over to her bed and placed it above a light-blue cotton skirt with an elastic waistband, smoothing down the fabric of both items with her hands, as if ironing. She frowned.

"Where did all my beautiful things go?" she asked Daughter, the room, the air. "My beautiful wrap dresses and my pencil skirts? I want to look my best for him. He's coming today, you know. Where are my lovely sheer blouses and my pantsuits? Have you seen them? Did you move them from my closet? Are you stealing from me?"

"No, Mama," Daughter said.

"I bought all of those things with my employee discount at Marshall Field's department store. You have no right to take them from me."

Daughter didn't remind Mama that Marshall Field's didn't exist anymore, and that she hadn't worked there since the eighties. Instead she gently led Mama away from the bed and into her recliner so she could eat. Mama's appetite was still solid. The doctor said that was a good thing, relatively speaking.

Mama chattered on as she busied herself buttering toast and adding ketchup to her eggs, something Daughter had always thought gross even though she liked both ketchup and eggs.

"He's coming today," Mama said between chews. Droplets of ketchup dotted the white ribbon on the front of her nightgown. Irrationally, this irked Daughter, and she made a mental note to put some stain remover on it before throwing it in the wash. Easily irked and forever trying to make order out of chaos, she was indeed her mother's daughter—the mother before this current mother. In some ways, Daughter preferred this current mother. In the oblivion of her mind, Mama was kinder—accusations of theft notwithstanding—and her needs were simpler.

Mama dabbed at her mouth with a paper towel. "Delicious. Thank you," she said in Daughter's general direction.

"You're welcome, Mama." Daughter was still getting used to such courtesy. She headed for the door. It was almost time for her first house showing of the day and for the home nurse to arrive and relieve her.

"You can come right back for this tray," Mama called after her. "I got to get ready. He'll be here shortly. Make sure you let me know when he's at the door, hear?"

Daughter heard, but she stood silent with her hand on the doorknob, her back to Mama.

"Did you hear me?" Mama's voice took on an edge of pleading. "Today's the day."

Daughter left the room and shut the door tight behind her.

—

As a kid during summer breaks from school, Daughter would sometimes whisper her real name to herself, just so she wouldn't go months at a time without hearing it. Everyone except her teachers followed Mama's lead and never called her by her name, always "Daughter," as if she existed only in relation to her mother, to her function in the family. *Daughter. Housekeeper. Cook. Babysitter. Nurse. Slave.* That's what she felt like. *Daughter, could you do this? Daughter, could you do that?* Which translated into: *You will do this. You will do that.* Without question or complaint, or else she got slapped. Meanwhile her brothers Rico and Bruce had been called by their given names and did only what they pleased.

Not much changed in their adulthood, only that Bruce was dead. Drugs. Rico, his wife, and kids lived on the other side of town. Daughter had to shame him into coming over on occasion to give her a break at least, even if he didn't care about spending time with Mama.

"Yo, she's gotta stop saying, 'Today is the day,' " Rico had complained to Daughter the first time Mama told him about Eddie Levert. "I don't want to keep hearing that crazy shit over and over again."

"I listen to it day in and day out," Daughter snapped. "You want to trade places?"

"You could hire someone full-time—"

"Or you could act like a son who gives a damn."

Rico crossed his arms and sighed. At forty, he still had a baby face and a perpetual pout.

"I shouldn't have to pay someone to sit with her when you're right here," Daughter had said. "I know she wasn't a perfect mother. But she is our mother."

"Don't lecture me about her," Rico said. Daughter knew that Mama didn't like Rico's wife, and the feeling was mutual, so she'd never gotten to know her grandkids. But Daughter had never asked Rico what it was like for him those two years between when she'd left home and when he left to join the air force. They had all been grieving Bruce's death in their own way. But whatever life with Mama was like for Rico after Daughter moved out, she couldn't imagine it being worse than what she endured: Mama had never laid a hand on Rico or Bruce.

"Fine. I won't lecture," Daughter had said. "Just . . . if Mama wants to talk about Eddie Levert, let her. She ain't hurtin' nobody, Rico."

At least not the way she used to.

—

The Bible says, "Train up a child in the way he should go, and when he is old he will not depart from it." In Mama's case, in her old age, she never spoke of the Bible. Instead she preached the gospel of the coming of Eddie Levert, lead singer of her favorite group back in the day, the O'Jays.

Both Eddie and Mama, son and daughter of the South, had had to bury their children, something even Daughter, who had never had kids, understood as especially cruel. Perhaps Mama had followed Eddie's life and career over the years and felt a special, unshakable bond with him.

In one of the family photo albums in Daughter's basement, there was a Polaroid picture of Mama with Eddie, taken in the seventies when the O'Jays came to town. Mama had somehow gotten backstage after the concert—Daughter had never been told the details—and took the picture, which Eddie signed. In the picture, Mama wore a low-cut, fire-red dress that hugged all her curves. Her hair, dyed a brassy reddish brown, had been hot combed and then curled into Farrah Fawcett flips. If not for her full nose and lips, she could've passed as a Farrah lookalike, as she was barely darker. Eddie was as dark as Mama was light. He wore a white suit, his chest bare, lapels wide. With his arm wrapped tight around Mama's tiny waist, Eddie grinned big at the camera. Mama grinned big at him. As a child, Daughter would pull out the album from time to time and stare at the photo, proof that Mama had once been happy.

When Daughter moved out at eighteen, it was partly because she feared Mama's unhappiness was contagious and partly because she was tired of being everyone's maid. Once she was out of the house, Daughter didn't walk away completely. There were no more slaps, no more wounding words, and from the outside looking in, Mama and Daughter could've been mistaken for close.

—

One Friday evening, Daughter and Mama sat at the kitchen table waiting for Rico to arrive. Daughter had shamed him into coming over for a few hours so she could go out to dinner with Tony, an old friend from high school. Tony stopped by from time to time to take care of things Daughter needed taken care of around the house. Including Daughter. The year before, after Mama had a second stroke and the doctor diagnosed her with vascular dementia, it was Tony, not Rico, who had helped Daughter pack up Mama's belongings and move her into Daughter's house.

When Tony arrived, Mama told him, "Today is the day. Eddie is coming."

Tony smiled at Mama and said, "Okay, young lady. I see you!"

Mama beamed and stood up to show Tony her outfit. "This is all I could find in that chiffo-robe to wear." She cut her eyes at Daughter, who just shook her head. "Do you think he will like it?"

"Oh, yes, ma'am!" Tony said, "If I was a few years younger, Eddie would have some competition on his hands."

"Oh, go on!" Mama said, blushing.

"It's been so long since I seen him," Mama said. With one hand, she tapped her tapered nails against the tabletop. With the other, she scratched her head. Daughter felt negligent; Mama was overdue for a wash and condition. Daughter would call her friend Tami in the morning to see if she could squeeze Mama in at her salon.

When Rico finally arrived, forty-five minutes late, Mama clapped and said, "There's my baby boy!"

Rico kissed Mama on the cheek, but rolled his eyes when she told him Eddie was coming. "Why is she scratching her head like that?" he asked Daughter with entirely too much bass and accusation in his voice.

"Don't." Daughter hissed at him in response. She turned to Mama. "Mama, Tony and I are going out. Rico is going to stay with you. I'll see you later."

"Okay," Mama said to the air. And to Tony: "You have a good time, young man."

Inside Tony's car, Daughter wept openly, and he rubbed her back and let her.

Once she had calmed to just sniffling, she said, "I'm sorry."

"For what?" Tony asked.

"For . . . all of that. I don't know where that came from."

"Maybe it came from the fact that you taking care of your mama and she doesn't even know who you are. But then Rico comes in, doesn't lift a finger to help without you asking, and it's all love from your mama. I'm just surprised it took you this long."

Daughter sobbed again. Tony started the car and began driving. "Dinner can wait," he said. "We can just drive, if you want."

Daughter nodded. "You know, even after I moved out, I was still there for her. After Bruce died, she threw herself into everything—children's church, Girl Scouts, Sunday School. And I drove her anytime she needed a ride. I took her to the grocery store every other week. I made sure she didn't spend Christmas, Easter, or Thanksgiving alone. Me! Not Rico. And now I'm taking care of her. Even after . . . even after how things were for me growing up. Trying to let bygones be bygones. I was there for her. And I still am. But for all she knows, I'm just another home nurse.

"And I try not to be an asshole like Rico about the whole Eddie Levert thing, but she cares more about that man than she does me! Every single day, it's the same thing. Sometimes I just want to scream, 'He's not coming! Ever!' " Daughter exhaled. "Is that terrible?"

Tony stroked his beard and tilted his head from side to side, like he was working out a kink in his neck.

"What?" Daughter asked.

"I don't want to speak out of turn . . ."

"Just say it."

"First, you need a break. And I don't mean this, us going out for dinner. You need a real break. A vacation. But more than that . . ." Tony sighed. "Look, I don't know what all went down when you were growing up. But you gotta make peace with it. I know that's easier said than done. But I think you have to find a way."

That's all I've ever done, Daughter thought but didn't say. Find a way to keep from upsetting Mama, find a way to keep Rico out of Mama's hair, find a way to get away from Mama, find a way to take care of herself with no help from Mama. Work low-wage job after low-wage job until she became a Realtor and found she had a knack for selling, buying, and flipping houses. And now a second job: take care of Mama. Daughter cursed under her breath.

"Like I said, I don't know what all went down . . ." Tony said.

"I'll tell you," Daughter said. "But let's go eat. I'm starving."

—

People in the neighborhood used to say that Mama kept pushing out babies until she got the color right. Daughter, her middle child, was darker than Bruce, the oldest, despite Daughter's father being lighter than Bruce's. Mama's third and last child, Ricardo, called Rico, fathered by a Puerto Rican musician who passed through one summer, was a buttery yellow baby boy with green eyes and sandy hair. His tight curls, thick lips, and broad nose meant that he could never pass. But passing wasn't the point. From what Daughter could piece together between her own observations and what she overheard Mama telling her friends, the point was that Rico had Mama's color. So for once the genetic dice had rolled in favor of the light-bright girl who believed dark niggas fucked the best of all. She played a kind of DNA roulette every time she brought one into her bed.

And then Mama got saved. It happened one Easter Sunday—they only went to church on Mother's Day, Christmas Eve, and Easter. On Mother's Day, Mama would wear a white flower pinned to her dress—Bruce called it The Dead Mama flower—and spend all day before and after church in her bedroom sobbing and missing her mother.

Daughter, Bruce, and Rico had few memories of their grandmother, a well-dressed, white-looking Black woman who had disowned their mother for having children out of wedlock. But she did come to visit a few times when they were growing up, always bearing bundles of toys, a crisp twenty-dollar bill for each of them, and for Mama, withering words about how she was living outside the will of God. Even as a child, Daughter understood her mama's tears on Mother's Day. She understood how your heart was still connected to your mama, even if she hurt you sometimes.

At first Daughter and her brothers felt joyful after Mama got saved, even though they didn't fully understand why. They were twelve, ten, and eight years old, and the best they could figure is that the church ladies who surrounded their mother as the pastor prayed had done some sort of magic. Mama had walked to the front of the church weeping during the altar call, but left the service smiling, her arms wrapped around her children, holding them close as they walked home. Mama's mama had died suddenly the year before—Daughter had overheard Mama say the word *aneurysm*, but didn't know what it meant. She'd also overheard Mama tell her friend Miss Lajene that she'd wished she'd gotten right with God before her mama died.

Unfortunately the zeal of the newly converted is bewildering to the children of the newly converted. One Saturday night, you've got every blanket in the house draped over your head to drown out the sound of your mother's headboard banging against your bedroom wall as she hollers her soon-to-be-ex-best friend's husband's name. And the next Saturday night, she's snatching the softened deck of playing cards from your hands because "Games of chance are from the devil!"

Daughter, with the logic of a ten-year-old,

thought she could understand how gin rummy might be from the devil, seeing as how the name of the game had *gin* in it. But what was wrong with "Knuckles" or "I Declare War," her and her brothers' other favorite games?

Some things changed about Mama A.C. (After Church, as Daughter thought of her). Like banning cards and men from the house. But some things didn't change. She still told Bruce and Rico to shut their mouths—and Daughter to shut her *Black* mouth—if they talked too loudly when her stories were on.

And the church was no match for Eddie Levert. The O'Jays were still Mama's favorite group, and Eddie Levert was still her favorite in the group. Mama B.C. (Before Church) would tell her girlfriends Miss Nancy and Miss Lajene, "Eddie Levert can have me any*time*, any*where*, and any*way* he want it, honey! You hear me?" And they would all fall out laughing.

Mama B.C. played O'Jays albums on Friday nights after dinner, if she didn't have a date or a card party to go to. She'd close her eyes, swing her hips, and sing along with the music. Her dance partners—a Kool cigarette and a glass of whisky, on the rocks. Johnnie Walker Red was her drink of choice.

On those Friday nights, Rico played DJ, changing the albums for Mama, while Daughter played bartender, adding ice and more liquor as needed, before Mama could ask for it. It was like a nightclub for one, with Mama getting lost in love songs and crying by night's end. Bruce would be out in the streets somewhere, staying out long enough to sneak in after Mama passed out on the couch, but before she woke up in the middle of the night to check on all of them and drag herself to bed.

As they entered their teen years, Bruce was the one out smoking dope, stealing, and brawling over crap games. But it was Daughter whom Mama warned, "Don't be out there showing your color!" on the rare occasions Daughter went out in the evenings.

Mama A.C. still spent her Friday nights with Eddie Levert, and she needed Daughter around to entertain Rico. Without a cigarette and a glass of whisky, Mama was free to wave her hands in the air as she sang, much like she did at church. In both places, Mama's nightclub for one and church, she was moved by the spirit to sway and eventually cry.

But over time, Daughter couldn't discern any joy in those tears. Mama's friends, Miss Nancy and Miss Lajene, remained "in the world," as Mama would say. So Mama distanced herself and soon lost touch. And the ladies at church who had surrounded Mama at the altar that Easter Sunday stopped calling after Mama finished the new member's class. Their work was done. They had led the poor unwed mother of three to the Living Water, as church folk referred to Jesus. But she wasn't their kind of people.

Years later Daughter wanted no part of the church or brown liquor because they had both made her mama cry.

—

When Daughter and Tony returned home from Red Lobster, Daughter paused at Mama's bedroom door and motioned for Tony to keep going down the hall to her bedroom. She cracked the door open just enough to see Mama curled up beneath her thin blanket and hear her snoring lightly. She closed the door and stopped to wash her hands in the bathroom once again, convinced they still smelled like crab.

In her bedroom, she found Tony already beneath her comforter. She undressed and slid in beside him. They had fallen into an easy groove with each other when Tony first started coming around, a decade earlier. He was thirty-two then, had been twice divorced, and was lonely. Daughter had never seen marriage or children in her future, had always been independent, and preferred her own company. Still, she had needs. Tony made her laugh and made her think. He was a generous lover and he was handy. For Daughter, that was enough.

Daughter tried to stay in the moment, to savor how alive her body felt next to Tony's. But her thoughts wandered to Mama. Always, Mama. Tony gripped her tighter and stroked her faster, as if he knew he was losing her. The headboard banged against the wall, and Daughter remembered how Mama B.C. didn't seem to care if her children heard her having sex. But the headboard banging had stopped when Mama found Jesus.

There's an old saying: mothers raise their daughters and love their sons. But who had ever loved Mama, besides her children? Despite her devotion to the church and chaste living, Mama had never had that peace that passes all understanding that was supposed to be yours when you invited Jesus into your heart. Nor did she have that joy, unspeakable joy, promised in the Scriptures. What Mama had was the love of Jesus—whose touch, Daughter imagined, was too ephemeral to quench anything—a quieter, more passive lover than the men she brought into her bed, but who nevertheless demanded everything.

—

The next morning after breakfast, Daughter asked Tony to sit with Mama for a little while.

Instead of calling the hair salon, she ran to Target and bought tearless baby shampoo and conditioner and everything else she would need to do Mama's hair herself.

After Tony left, Daughter explained to Mama that she was going to wash her hair. Mama could still shower alone and dress herself, so Daughter, wanting to respect her privacy, asked whether she would mind leaning over the kitchen sink.

"Well . . . I don't know." Mama patted her hair. It was mostly white now, too thin for the Farrah Fawcett flips, but still hung to her shoulders. "Do you think Eddie would like it? He's coming today, you know."

"Yes, Mama. I know." Daughter swallowed the lump in her throat. "And I think Eddie would want you to let me wash your hair over the sink."

"Well, all right then."

It took a few tries to get the water temperature just right. Daughter had lots of towels on hand so Mama could pause and wipe her face whenever she needed to.

When they finished washing and conditioning, she took Mama back to Mama's room to change into a dry shirt. Then Daughter sat Mama at her vanity table and stood behind her to blow-dry her hair. Mama smiled into the mirror.

As Daughter parted Mama's hair into sections, taking her time to oil each section and massage the scalp, Mama sighed and leaned back into Daughter's middle.

"You know, Mama," Daughter began. "Eddie called and told me he's going to be late."

"Oh, no!" Mama said.

"But he doesn't want you to worry. He wants you to know you're in good hands with me. He said, 'Now you take good care of her until I get there, Daughter.' "

"Daughter?"

"Yes, Mama. It's me. Daughter."

"And what else did Eddie say?"

"He said . . . 'You tell her I'm coming and take good care of her.' And I said, 'Yes, sir. I will tell her.' "

"You always were such a polite girl," Mama said. She reached up and patted Daughter's hand.

"You remember me, Mama?"

"Sure I do!"

Daughter began to tear up, but also couldn't help but smile. She didn't know whether Mama remembered her. But it was enough to know that Mama wanted her to believe she did.

She continued massaging Mama's scalp. "Does that feel good?"

"Mmm-hmmm," Mama said, over and over until it turned into humming, a random tune Daughter didn't recognize.

Daughter looked at the two of them in the mirror. Light and dark, but an otherwise matching set of round faces and big, brown eyes stared back at her. Mama's scalp was still pale, but the rest of her had darkened over time. She was still lighter than a paper bag, she might've bragged, if her mind still fixated on such things.

"Mama, a long time ago, you were real hard on me. Real hard. And I don't know if you remember any of that. Part of me hopes you remember, because I can't forget. But then, if you remember, I wish you would apologize, or at least recognize . . ."

Mama kept humming. Then she said, "You know when Eddie sang about having a lot of loves, I was one of them loves." Mama poked at her chest. "Me. Lil nobody me." Mama chuckled to herself. "Eddie loved me once upon a time. That one night."

"You're not a nobody, Mama."

"Oh, yeah? Well, who am I, then?" Mama sounded so lucid, it startled Daughter. As if someone else had come into the room with them.

"You're . . . someone who can't give me what I need. But you're not nobody."

"Yeah?"

"Yeah."

Daughter twisted Mama's hair into a single braid. Then she laid out a new turquoise sundress on the bed for her to put on.

"I'll step out and let you get dressed. And I'll bring your lunch when I come back."

"That would be nice," Mama said. "I want to be ready when Eddie comes. Today's the day."

When Daughter returned with Mama's lunch tray, Mama was in her recliner, smoothing her hands over the sundress, smiling. "I look beautiful," she said.

"Yes, you do," Daughter said. She placed the tray on Mama's lap.

Mama picked up the Polaroid next to her sandwich plate. She stared at it for a moment before putting it down and picking up her sandwich.

Daughter sighed and played the song she'd cued up on her cell phone. As the opening chords of the O'Jays' "Forever Mine" filled the room, she expected some flicker of recognition from Mama, a smile or something. But there was nothing. Even when Eddie came in on the third verse, it didn't seem to register with Mama that this was the same song she had quoted earlier. The song played on. Daughter wasn't sure whether Mama was even listening. Mama ate her sandwich and fruit salad, the Polaroid forgotten.

And then, as Eddie begged his lover to stay, Mama picked up the photo and began to sing along with him, her voice strong and certain.

ACKNOWLEDGMENTS

THIS COLLECTION took shape over the course of many years and twists and turns, and I appreciate everyone who has been along for the ride. Thanks for your love, friendship, support, pep talks, advice, meals, late-night laughter, technical help, feedback, dance breaks, and unwavering belief in me and my stories: Chris Ivey, Tyrese Coleman, Fran and Alan Edmunds, Renee Simms, Bassey Ikpi, Faith Adiele, Lonnae O'Neal, Stanley Love Tate, James Bernard Short, Diana Veiga, Khaliah Williams, Danielle Evans, David Haynes and the whole Kimbilio Center for African American Fiction family, Teresa Foley, Aaliyah Thomas, Melanie Dione, Adam Smyer, Dr. DeMarquis Clarke, Damon Young, Chanie Infante Louisma, Doug Anthony, Tony Burroughs, Wade Carver, Quake Pletcher, Eyan Spaulding, Harry Weaver III, Daniel Henry, Alison Kinney, Mark Sequeira, Rev. Maxwell Grant, Bomani Jones, Mat

Johnson, Amber Edmunds, Renelle Carrington, Toya Smith, Celeste C. Smith, Bernadette Adams Davis, Swati Khurana, Meredith Driscoll, Carolyn Edgar, Lawrence Wagner, and Sekou Campbell.

Big thanks to Derek Krissoff, Sara Georgi, Jeremy Wang-Iverson, Sarah Munroe, Charlotte Vester, and the whole team at West Virginia University Press for giving this collection so much enthusiastic support and care.

Shout out to my Day Ones: Tamara Winfrey Harris, Yona Harvey, Taneshia Nash Laird, Rebecca Lusolo, Genie Maples, and Issa Mas (my Celie!). Y'all got me this far. Thank you and I love you!

Special thanks and love to my thoughtful readers, cheerleading squad supreme, and dear friends: Brian Broome, Asha Rajan, Abeer Hoque, Mimi Watkins, George Kevin Jordan, Samantha Irby, and Kiese Laymon.

Dennis Norris II, thank you for all the tea and friendship, and for loving and publishing the very first story ("Eula") in what would become this collection.

Many thanks also to the editors of *Cheat River Review*, *Baltimore Review*, and *Barrelhouse Magazine* for publishing previous versions of some of these stories.

And thanks to Ansel Elkins for the "Autobiography of Eve." This poem is a treasure.

Love and gratitude to Vanessa German for

countless gifts and graces and encouragements. You make the world better.

Thank you for the love and the laughs: Dr. Tyffani Dent, DeShong Perry, Dr. Carolyn Strong, and Dr. LaTasha Sturdivant.

Thank you to my agent extraordinaire, Danielle Chiotti, for first envisioning this collection and guiding me every step of the way to the finish line.

Thank you, Laura Szabo-Cohen and Tony Norman, for being awesome mentors and friends. Twenty-plus years, that's a mighty long time . . .

To my sisters—Donnette, Shalawn, Tiffany, and Felicia—our story is just beginning.

Thank you, Taylor and Peyton, for your patience and for being proud of me. I love you!

Finally, thank you to my mama and Nay-Nay for sending me to church and Sunday School all those years. I miss you every day.